DANGER FOR DAISY

Mature student Daisy Morgan plucks up her courage to attend a get-together — only to cannon straight into a handsome gentleman, spilling her drink all over his smart suit into the bargain! To make matters worse, he turns out to be Seth, her flatmates' archaeologist friend. After this unconventional meeting, sparks quickly kindle between the pair, and Daisy accompanies Seth to a dig on a remote island. But danger lurks on Sealfarne — and they are about to unearth it . . .

FRANCESCA CAPALDI

◆

DANGER
FOR DAISY

Complete and Unabridged

LINFORD
Leicester

First published in Great Britain in 2018

First Linford Edition
published 2020

A catalogue record for this book is available
from the British Library.

ISBN 978–1–4448–4554–9

Published by
Ulverscroft Limited
Anstey, Leicestershire

Set by Words & Graphics Ltd.
Anstey, Leicestershire
Printed and bound in Great Britain by
T. J. International Ltd., Padstow, Cornwall

This book is printed on acid-free paper

1

Daisy Morgan pulled her coat around her as she strode down the busy London pavement. There'd been drizzle in the air since darkness had fallen and, while the weather had been mild for the time of year, the incessant damp chilled her.

It wasn't Christmas weather at all. But then, the whole atmosphere was different in the city. Not like being back at home with her parents in Cambridgeshire, each house in her friendly street on the outskirts of Huntingdon blazing with festive lights. There were Santas on every corner here, window displays full of lights and baubles and tinsel, yet it all felt artificial.

'Oh, sorry,' she said, as a thick-set jogger knocked into her, sprinting past without looking. She rubbed her arm, shaking her head as he ignored her and disappeared into the crowd.

People were so unfriendly in the city. She turned to move on, but her eye was caught by the book shop display. She needed to get a present for Matt. Something that said *we're friends* but not *let's get back together*. Even though she'd have liked to. Maybe. But that ship seemed to have sailed, especially in the three months since she'd started uni as a slightly mature student.

She felt an empty space deep inside herself. She'd spent some part of Christmas Day with him every year since she was sixteen. Eight years. Should she buy him books while she was here? No, she was stalling. Right. Bar Splendido.

Five minutes later she stood outside the bar, her stomach churning as she considered its entrance. Stupid to be frightened of going in on her own. Her flatmates would be in there. But what if they hadn't arrived yet and she had to sit on her own? *Oh, just go in, you great big baby!*

Right. One foot in front of the other. She took a deep breath and hauled

2

open the heavy door.

It was cavernous inside, nooks and crannies all over the place, each dimly lit with coloured fairy lights. There were no other signs of seasonal decorations, just the thumping strains of ancient Christmas hits and people shouting to be heard. She'd have to search the place. Left? Right?

She chose right and set off with purpose, not noticing the guy until there was an, 'Oof! Careful!'

What had just happened? Oh no, she'd knocked his drink and it had gone all over his very smart, and in all likelihood expensive, suit. What a careless clot she was!

'I'm so sorry,' she said, as he brushed at the drops on the lapel. She took a tissue from her bag and started dabbing at the jacket, noting the quality of the fabric.

'Please don't do that, thank you.'

A strange expression clouded his features and she thought he was going to start shouting at her, so odd was his look — and yet, so breathtakingly striking with his wavy chestnut hair and large green eyes, full mouth and dimpled chin. It was as if the crowds around her had freeze-framed and her body had melted.

She shook herself. 'Can I buy you a new drink? Pay for your cleaning bill? Or . . . ' Her mouth went dry as she ran out of suggestions.

He stared at her, mouth slightly open. Then his face relaxed to the point of having no expression at all.

'I'm fine. Excuse me.' He put the now empty glass on the bar, calling to the barman, 'Sorry, there's a spillage on the floor, here.' He pointed to where she was still standing, then headed to the men's room, shoving the door open.

Daisy stumbled blindly past the bar — left this time — her heart crashing against her ribs, her brain in no fit state to advise her what to do next.

★ ★ ★

4

Had he been a little hard on her?

Seth squeezed the soap out of the dispenser before washing his hands, considering the young woman who'd knocked beer down his suit. He dabbed at it after rinsing his hands, making a mental note to take it to the dry cleaners as soon as possible. He pictured her long copper hair and the contrasting eyes, the colour of a conker shell. Pretty. Yeah . . . pretty clumsy. He chuckled to himself as he reached for a paper towel. She'd rather blindsided him, taking his breath away as she appeared out of nowhere like a . . . What? He hadn't quite formulated the answer to that, feeling the power of . . . something.

So much for his reputation as an intelligent and intuitive academic! This young woman had robbed him of his wits and he'd probably never even see her again. He stopped drying his hands, standing there like a statue, as an intense sadness overwhelmed him.

He threw the paper towel in the bin. *Don't be so daft, man,* he said silently to his reflection, noting how tired he looked. As if she'd have looked twice at him with those dark circles under his eyes and his hair badly needing a cut.

He'd barely had time to shave the sprouting stubble when he'd arrived in London from Crete this morning, only glad that his sister had managed to send down the suit, shirt, tie and shoes he'd requested to the house of his old uni friend, Freddie. He'd been able to change there before they'd headed out to lunch together.

Freddie had recently got married — a big affair Seth had managed to get to before heading for Crete. Bridesmaids and banquets, rings and churches, houses to buy and someone else to think about — he didn't envy Freddie. He wasn't ready for such a commitment.

The rumble of voices and music increased as two men crashed through the door, laughing. Time to get back to his friends.

★ ★ ★

'Daisy? Dais!'

There was maybe a second's lapse before she realised it was her name being called. She spun round, looking for the source.

'Here, Dais!'

Callie. What a relief! And Dave, Bea and Toby. She sucked in air and let out a shuddering sigh.

'What on earth is wrong?' said Bea as Daisy plonked herself on a stool. 'You're bright pink.'

'Oh, dear.' She clasped her cheeks with her palms and shook her head. 'I just bumped into this totally stunning guy and spilled his drink down him. You know, the usual idiot thing I tend to do.'

'Hey, girlfriend, don't put yourself down all the time.'

That was easy for Bea to say, with her elegantly tailored trousers and sophisticated top, her neat little bob. And there was Callie, who could carry off bohemian in her radiant, couldn't-give-a-damn way. All four of her flatmates

7

were older and immeasurably more savvy than her. She always felt like the hick from the sticks next to them.

'The Doc's being a long time,' said Dave. 'He was only supposed to be getting himself a drink.'

Daisy screwed up her eyes. 'The Doc?'

'Yeah, a mate of mine and Cal's. He's coming to crash over Christmas so he'll be able to join in Callie's birthday party tomorrow. We first met him when we were backpacking in Turkey.'

'I didn't know anyone was staying.'

'Sorry, we should have asked. We didn't know ourselves until this afternoon,' said Callie. 'He rang Dave out of the blue.'

Despite her pique at having a stranger in the house, she envied this guest she'd never met. What would it be like just to do things because you wanted to? Just turn up somewhere, go off somewhere else.

Leaving home to come to uni was the most daring thing she'd ever done — and

8

she'd taken six years longer than most people even to do that. After working all that time for her father, she'd finally gone against her boyfriend's wishes and applied to University College to do biological sciences.

'Loved that suit he was wearing,' said Bea, a grin lighting up her face. 'It clung in all the right places.'

Daisy felt the faded blush blossom once more. It would have been a good description of the stranger who — oh, no . . . surely not . . .

'Hi, sorry I've been so long. What the — You?'

The guy she'd bumped into, the guy who still had a wet patch on the lapel of his lovely suit, was standing open mouthed, staring at her.

Oh floor, swallow me up now, please!

2

Toby asked the new arrival, 'What's that down your threads, Doc? And where's your drink?'

Bea's laugh rang out and it was only a moment later the others caught on and joined in.

'So this is the totally — ?' started Bea.

' — silly accident I just had. Yes. My bad,' Daisy put in quickly, her voice rising to a squeak.

Callie stood up. 'Seth, meet our flat-mate, Daisy. Daisy — Seth. Intros done.'

'You mean Doctor Seth Simkin,' said Dave in a mock serious tone.

'Shuddup Dave,' said Seth. 'I'm off duty.'

His hand went out reluctantly and Daisy shook it. His skin was warm, soft . . . so soft. He pulled his hand away abruptly.

Doctor. As in medical? Research? Either

way, she already felt an idiot without him turning out to be immensely qualified.

'I am honestly, most humbly sorry,' said Daisy, who was holding down the urge to burst into tears. How lame would that look? Typical of her, though — the first guy since September who'd sparked any interest in her, and she'd made a fool of herself. As per. And to think she'd considered uni a new start, a chance to throw off her self-doubt and get a sense of direction. The possibility of it still quickened her heart, still created that deep tingle of hope in her belly.

'Apology accepted,' said Seth, looking at the ground. 'I'll get us both a drink.'

'No, I should get — '

'What do you want?' he said, discussion on the matter clearly unwelcome.

'Cider, please. Draught. Or bottled. Whatever they have really.' She shrugged.

'Right.' His tall, lean frame disappeared into the crowd.

Blast, blast, blast! What difference did it make? It wasn't as if Seth would ever

11

look twice at her, other than to convey what a total numb-brain she was. Bea would be more his style, or Callie, but they were hooked up with Toby and Dave. Here was she in her old jeans and the Shetland jumper Matt bought her three Christmases ago — and just look at her scruffy trainers! She stuck her foot out a little to get a better view, frowning, twirling a lock of her hair round her index finger.

Toby nudged her. 'What's wrong with you?'

'Hmm? Sorry. Just thinking about things we need to do for the party tomorrow . . . and Christmas.'

A little white lie, but she could hardly confess her real thoughts. She looked past the crowd towards the bar, dreading the return of 'Dr Seth Simkin', yet yearning for it at the same time.

Seth returned ten minutes later, his mouth down at the corners. He barely grunted an acknowledgment and avoided eye contact as she thanked him for the drink.

Was he going to be a wet blanket his whole visit? The eager anticipation she'd felt for her first Christmas away from home diminished.

'Busy, was it?' Dave asked him.

'Yep. Not had to deal with crowds like this the last month I've been in Crete. Then again, they didn't serve real ale there, so it's not all bad.' His laugh lit up his face, his whole manner animated in a way it hadn't been moments earlier.

She sighed, thankful that the din of the bar covered it. As she breathed out, shockwaves flooded her body. What on earth was going on here? She'd never felt such a thing in her life. Not with Matt. Not with anyone.

'Were you going to say something?' Dave asked her.

'Me?' Had she been staring? Of course she had! 'Um. What were you doing in Crete, Seth?' At least her brain kicked in with something sensible.

He searched her face for some seconds before his head jerked back a tiny amount and a look of surprise suggested she'd just materialised in front of him. She wondered what snidey thing he'd reply with, but the fractious attitude didn't return. His lips lifted into a generous smile once more. Oh dear. She was in danger of spontaneously combusting as it was!

'I was on a dig. I'm an archaeologist and senior lecturer with the University of Northumberland.'

'Really,' she said, hoping that would be a sufficient reply, beset with her usual inadequacies. What could she say to such a person?

She was grateful to Callie for filling the space with more details of how she and Dave had met Seth on one of their backpacking tours, when they'd stopped off to volunteer at a dig. At the end of the account, Daisy said, 'I thought you must be a businessman, what with the suit.'

She felt an astonishing amount of relief that he wasn't. Matt's foray into the business world had changed him.

He'd set up his own company eight years ago and it had been a runaway success. He'd started indulging in designer gear, frequenting top restaurants and 'members only' clubs. Was it any wonder he'd had increasingly little time for her?

Seth grimaced. 'Perish the thought,' he said, searching her face as if he'd met her before but couldn't work out where. 'I'd just had a business lunch with an old friend. He wanted to go a bit upmarket.'

He took a drink of his beer and she wondered if he wasn't so different to Matt after all.

'Personally I'd have been happy with pizza, but he was paying, so it was his call.' He laughed. No, not like Matt at all. He licked his top lip before saying, 'So what do you do?'

'I'm doing biology at University College.'

'What do you want to do with it?'

She tried to think of a good answer but realised she didn't have one. 'I don't know. I liked biology best at school. It was that or history . . . that's it.'

He nodded but said nothing. This made her feel even more of a dummy. What was she going to talk about with this man over Christmas?

Then he smiled at her again and she felt a rushing sensation that climbed from her feet to her brain, making her light-headed. They had never met before, and yet she felt she'd been holding him deep inside her soul all her life.

'Bit like me at one time then,' he said.

Perhaps Christmas wouldn't be so bad after all.

★ ★ ★

The next morning, Daisy was having a ball larking around with her friends, putting up the decorations with Callie and Bea. At her parents' home, tinsel was declared untidy and forbidden,

16

though she always sneaked some into her bedroom to wrap around her headboard, as did her sister.

Oh dear, her sister. Her biggest regret was that she'd upset Hannah when she'd announced she was spending Christmas with her friends. Still — no doubt it wouldn't be long before Hannah wanted to spread her wings too.

Daisy picked up the last piece of tinsel from the dining table, weaving it round the back of a chair. From the galley kitchen, a tenor voice was belting out *I Believe in Father Christmas*.

'Pass that bag on the table, would you, Dais?' said Callie, standing on a chair in front of the bookcase. 'I've run out of tinsel here.'

'There's more? Fab!' She handed a piece up to Callie. 'There's a divine aroma of bacon wafting out of the kitchen. What's Seth up to?'

The three of them turned to look through the open door to the kitchen. Steam was issuing forth and there was a distinct whiff of garlic.

'Seth's cooking some of the food for Cal's party this evening,' said Bea. 'He was out before we got up to buy ingredients.'

'He cooks?' Daisy was wide-eyed at the thought.

'Why the surprise? He's a darned good cook,' said Callie. 'You should have tasted some of the stuff he produced on the dig in Turkey.'

Matt had always refused to cook anything on principle. He said he had better things to do. Presumably she'd have got lumbered with it all if they'd got married or moved in together. Or he'd have hired a cook. That would be more his style these days. A part of her still wondered what it would be like to share a house with him.

Seth stuck his head round the door.

'Breakfast is ready for the hungry workers. Where are Dave and Toby?'

'Decorating the living room,' said Callie, jumping off the stool. 'Should have known you were doing breakfast. You're a star.' She headed over to the

18

kitchen door and kissed his cheek.

Daisy's stomach whooshed as she imagined it was she who'd just done that. Not likely. She'd only known him — she looked at the clock — about thirteen hours, but she wouldn't have done it if she'd known him for a year.

'I'll get the others,' said Daisy, feeling like the Cowardly Lion and wishing there was some kind of Yellow Brick Road she could skip down to find the courage she always lacked.

You stood your ground and went to uni.

Yes, but at the cost of her relationship. It had been slipping downhill for a year since she told Matt she was applying. But surely, if he'd really loved her, he wouldn't have been so . . . so off with her wanting to continue her education. *He* hadn't needed to, he'd countered. No — but he'd fallen on his feet with the business.

She opened the glass door between the dining room and living room. Dave and Toby were leaning over the hi-fi unit, looking at something.

'Breakfast is served,' she called.

'Is Seth at it again?' said Dave. 'Wonderful. Hope he's done his scrambled egg special.'

They took their seats at the table with much fuss and laughter, finally settling down.

'So, when do you want your presents, Callie?' said Seth, serving her and Daisy with plates full of scrambled egg with smoked salmon.

'Later, when we're dressed for the party. I do love having a birthday at this time of the year. Though I don't relish this creeping towards my thirties lark.'

'Join the club!' said Dave. 'Well, apart from Daisy here, who's the baby.'

Now there was a label she could do without. She always felt like the baby.

Seth laughed 'I must be the old man then.'

'How old are you?' Daisy asked, regretting it immediately, but confused by his statement.

'Only twenty-nine, but still the

oldest,' he replied. 'Now eat up so we can get breakfast over and done with. I've got some flans to make for this party.'

'You're incorrigible, Seth,' Callie called as he hurried back to the kitchen.

A pile of Callie and Dave's friends were coming over later to the party. Daisy knew it would be fun. Maybe she'd even make some new friends. At the same time there was that familiar lump in her chest. Crowds of unknown people made her want to run away. She'd always been like that. Being with someone as confident as Matt had meant she'd never been alone in these situations.

Until she'd started uni. She'd found a few people to hang out with, but they were acquaintances rather than friends.

Seth returned with one more plate, putting it down in the empty spot next to Daisy, where he sat down. He was dressed casually today, slim jeans and a checked shirt, his hair flopping forward instead of being slicked neatly back. He was even more stunning.

Callie jumped up. 'Forgot to get the juice out.'

When she'd disappeared Dave, on the other side of Seth, took his arm, whispering, 'Are you going to vacate the kitchen for a while later on, only Daisy's going to make Cal's birthday cake.'

'She cooks?' he said, eyebrows raised as he surveyed Daisy.

Bea burst out laughing and Daisy followed a second later, thinking how funny it was that she'd said the same about him. Bea must think so too . . . Oh, no. He might have said it because he overheard what she said. She felt her ears go pink and willed her face not to follow suit.

'What's so funny?' said Callie, returning.

'Nothing, my darling, nothing,' said Dave.

Seth half smiled at Daisy so that she was left in no doubt he had heard the earlier conversation.

Seth was still busy cooking flans when Daisy wanted to get in the kitchen. He cheerfully shifted his ingredients and utensils along to share the narrow galley worktop, though he was already pushed for space. Every now and then he peeped round, examining what she was doing, until she gave him a shy look and put an arm around her bowl, like a school kid with an exam paper.

Seth couldn't deny that he experienced a small thrill as they shuffled past each other several times. He could put up with the inconvenience for that. He really needed to get out of work more.

He noticed her place three cake tins on the hob as he washed up the items he'd used. Lifting the bowl from the mixer she poured a dark brown batter into one of the tins before placing lighter brown and yellow batters into the other tins from two other bowls.

'I'll need the oven in a few minutes,' she said.

'Don't worry, I'll be out of your hair soon.' As he wiped his hands on a towel, the oven beeper went off. 'There. Right on cue.' He took two baked flans from the oven, placing them on a baking tray on the stove. 'Would you like any help now I'm done?'

'Only to wash up . . . no, I'm kidding. I'll do it in a minute.'

'I don't mind doing yours along with mine.'

'Honestly, I was joking.' She glanced at various bowls she'd used, looked back at him and smiled.

'You should learn to wash up as you go along,' said Seth. 'Makes it easier at the end.'

She tutted. 'Yes, thank you Gordon Ramsay.'

'He probably has people to wash up for him.'

Her silence made him fear he'd offended her by poking his nose in. Her sudden laughter reassured him, but also troubled him. That was a weird sensation that just passed through him.

'Go on. I'll put these in the oven, then you can wash, I'll dry,' Daisy said.

'My pleasure.' He rolled his arm and bowed.

Cakes cooking, she whipped the tea towel off the handle of the oven door and started drying.

'So, how come you're not going home for Christmas?' he said.

She pursed her lips convincing him that he'd definitely said the wrong thing this time.

'Why aren't you, come to that?'

'I live on my own,' he said. 'Not a very interesting reason. Dave said you weren't going to your folks as you'd originally planned, so . . . sorry, I'm being nosy, aren't I?'

'Yes. And don't you have parents and other family, even if you do have your own pla — oh, sorry . . . they might have passed on.'

'No, nothing like that. My sister's spending Christmas with her husband's family and Mum and Dad have gone to Australia, backpacking.'

'Backpacking? Wow! I couldn't imagine my parents doing that in any universe. My parents like B&Bs in the countryside.' She exhaled a little 'Huh!' as if to say *What are they like?*

'Sometimes I wish mine did!' he replied. 'I worry about them.'

She laughed. 'Aren't they supposed to worry about you? No girlfriend or significant other to hang out with then?' She coughed and turned slightly away.

'Nope. You?'

'Well, there was . . . not now. In fact, he'll be around, at home, 'cos his parents only live up the road and are friends with mine so . . . Anyway, I'm going home at New Year instead as I know Matt's going skiing then.'

'Ah. The awkward ex.'

'Not exactly. But we'd been going out since I was sixteen and he was eighteen, and we've known each other all our lives. It sort of came to a natural end and now we're kind of like brother and sister.'

'It can happen with young love.'

'When he left school he started his own business, became successful. I worked for my dad after leaving. It was five years before I decided to apply to uni. A student to his successful business-man.'

'How old are you?'

'Twenty-four. Late starter. But that's a story for another time.'

He emptied the washing-up water out.

'What, when we're washing up together some time in the future?' He liked that idea. Liked it maybe a little too much.

'It's just an expression.'

He dried his hands. 'Pity,' he said, as he strolled out of the kitchen.

★ ★ ★

That was it, the bit she feared about cake making was over — she'd written on top of the ganache in white choco-late icing *Happy 28th Birthday Callie* and she hadn't made one mistake. Dave had taken Callie out to choose a present, despite her protests of wanting to get ready, so Daisy could ice in secret. She was still admiring her handiwork when Seth shuffled into the kitchen with several cups hanging on the fingers of both hands. He put them down on the draining board and turned to inspect her finished product.

'Wow, that's impressive. Worthy of *Bake Off*. You must have a steady hand. Did you do cookery evening classes?'

'No. I just have an interest and used to have plenty of time to pursue it, I guess.' She chewed her bottom lip, feeling vaguely uncomfortable with the compliment. 'You're a bit of a mean chef yourself. These flans look tasty.'

'I'm quite good, I'll admit, but this is something else. Where are you going to hide it?'

'Hide it? Oh, good point! The only place is in my bedroom, I guess. How on earth will I get it up there without dropping it?'

'I'll give you a hand. Do you want to clean up first?' He pointed to her face.

She lifted a pan lid to use as a mirror.

Sure enough, she'd got icing down one cheek. How on earth had she managed that? 'I'll do it after.'

Daisy was nervous all the way up the stairs as she and Seth tried to keep the cake level. Finally in the bedroom she steered him towards the chest of drawers, which, for a change, had an almost clear surface.

'I see you lucked out with the box room,' Seth chuckled, looking around.

'I couldn't expect a couple to sleep in here, now could I?'

'No. True. What if you get hooked up?'

'I guess it'll be cosy,' she replied, blushing furiously. 'But really, I've no plans for that in the near future.'

He pointed at the poster on her wall. 'Led Zeppelin. Retro. I like it. I'm a big fan.'

Seth's gaze did a circuit of the room.

'Yes, I know it's untidy. I was going to clean up before Christmas.'

Seth lifted his hands, palms outward. 'I didn't say a thing.'

'You didn't have to.'

'I've been on enough digs to train myself to be tidy. You can't be messy, living in a tent.'

'I'm sure I could,' she laughed. 'In fact, I know I could. I've been camping a couple of times with the Guides.'

'Did you like it?'

'Yeah. It was fun. All mucking in together.'

'With the emphasis on muck?'

'Ha ha!'

His mouth opened as if about to add something, when the doorbell rang out *Jingle Bells*.

'Sorry, Dave set it up to play that,' said Daisy. 'He thinks it's funny. I'd better answer it.'

'You clean yourself up. I'll answer it. Perhaps Dave and Callie forgot their key.'

She was relieved not to have to go to the door in that state. She looked down at the apron. She tutted, untying the item and rolling it in a ball to put in her laundry basket. She headed to the bathroom to wash her face and hands, leaving the door ajar in case it was the postman and she needed to sign for a parcel. She'd just splashed water on her face when she saw Seth in the doorway, his eyes narrowed.

She reached for her towel, rubbing away the water. 'Who is it?'

'It's your boyfriend, Matt.'

3

Matt sat patiently out of the way with a newspaper after Daisy explained she needed to get things ready, getting up only to be introduced to her flatmates as they each appeared. She assumed Matt and Seth had already introduced themselves.

When she appeared down the stairs after getting changed, ten minutes before the party was due to start, Seth was about to head up.

'Nice dress. You're rocking that Boho look.' He waved his hand up and down to take in the outfit.

She reached the bottom step feeling ridiculously pleased, like a kid who'd just met the pop star she had a huge crush on. 'Thanks. It's Bea's, but she persuaded me to wear it. She said none of my clothes were party-ish enough.'

'She made a great choice. Have a good party.'

'Aren't you staying for it?'

'Yep, but I don't suppose I'll see much of you.'

He pointed up the stairs and she took that as a hint she was in the way.

'Sorry.' She came down and into the hallway a few steps.

'For what?'

'Being in your way.'

He voiced a brief, 'Ah,' before taking the stairs two at a time.

When she entered the living room, Matt leapt to his feet, coming to her and taking her hand.

The first guest arrived a moment later.

From that moment, Matt didn't let go of her. He made polite conversation with everyone, Daisy a tiny step behind him, nodding and smiling in the way she always did when out with him. The old sensation of comfort returned to her. She felt safe with him as he buffered her against the world. Hadn't she often imagined a scene like this, as she'd lain awake the last few months wondering if she'd done the right thing?

She was aware of Seth flitting from person to person, beer glass in hand, chatting with good humour. He was ignoring her. Or was that her perception because she'd wanted to impress him? Oh yes, she had, she realised that. She felt daft now, not for her instant teenage-like crush on Seth, but because having just told him it was over with Matt, she was here holding hands with him. She hoped Seth didn't think she'd been trying to deceive him.

Had his *Don't suppose I'll see much of you* been tinged with regret or was had it been just a statement of fact?

'Didn't we, dear?'

'Mm? Sorry?' What had Matt just said that she was supposed to agree with?

'Honestly, Daisy, how do you ever concentrate in those lectures of yours?' Matt turned to Toby. 'Always been a bit away with the fairies, our Daisy. I wonder how she even got her A levels sometimes.' He laughed heartily.

Toby glanced at her, widening his

eyes. 'Must circulate. Interesting to meet you at last, Matt.' He glanced once more at Daisy before moving on.

Matt seemed oblivious to the silent exchange. 'I suppose he's what you'd call a hipster, with the beard and all.'

'I'm not sure he sees himself as anything in particular.'

Matt pulled Daisy close to whisper, 'Can we go somewhere quieter to talk?'

'I'd rather stay, if you don't mind,' she said.

'Only out to the hall for a few minutes.'

If she said no, he'd only keep on. 'Just a few minutes then.'

Once in the hall he put his arms around her. 'I've been such an idiot, Daisy, letting you go.'

'Letting me go? I didn't need your permission to come to uni.'

'I mean, letting our relationship go. I was so afraid of losing you if you left that I ended up doing just that. Think of all the lovely things we could do together over the holidays. I could take

35

you to the sales and treat you.' He looked down at her dress and frowned. 'I could buy you something that really suits you, not like that dress.'

The opening bars of *Blue Christmas* started in the other room.

'Let's dance, Matt. Come on.' She pulled on his arm. 'Give me time to think about things.'

'I knew you'd see sense.'

He followed her and they started dancing straight away, giving Daisy a chance to look round. All the guests were older than her, more sophisticated. Seth was bound to hook up with someone here. As she saw him walk to the makeshift dance floor with a friend of Callie's she knew what she was feeling was jealousy.

She looked away. Matt was talking about the business, how well he was doing, schmoozing with bigwigs. She was little Daisy again, the hick from the sticks. She didn't fit into either Matt's or Seth's worlds. The thought made her queasy.

The woman who asked Seth to dance was very pleasant. Anna she was called. They were having an interesting chat together about his job and hers at the British Museum as an archivist. They had much in common. But there was no sparkle.

He'd glanced at Daisy and Matt several times during the dance as he and Anna chatted. He noted Matt's black hair, long on top and shaved at the sides, slicked back, the dark, beady eyes and haughty demeanour. And what was with the suit for a casual party? But then, he might not have known about the do.

When the song had finished Seth excused himself to Anna, saying he had to talk to Dave about something and that it had been lovely to meet her. Since Dave was preoccupied with Callie, and he came across Toby in the dining room, he stopped to talk to him instead.

Seth leaned in to be heard over the

37

music. 'Is it just me, or is that Matt a bit of a slime ball?'

'You're just jealous, mate,' said Toby.

'Why would I be jealous? I only just met Daisy.'

Toby gave him a look.

'Body language. You're well into her.'

'Is this the psychologist in you talking?'

'Yep. Anyway, you're right about him. I'm not surprised Daisy escaped to London. He has her right under his thumb. He was so condescending to her when I spoke to them, like she was a silly little girl.'

'You'd not met him before?' asked Seth.

'Nah. I was under the impression they'd split up completely. It's one of the reasons Daisy wanted to stay here for Christmas 'cos their folks are good friends and she'd end up seeing a lot of him and didn't want to.'

'I see . . .'

'By the way, the psychologist in me's noticed her body language, too.'

Seth wasn't sure he wanted to know,

but he asked all the same. 'And?'

'And she's well into you, too, mate. Or was until Matt turned up.'

'For all the good it'll do me now,' he muttered as he headed for the refuge of the kitchen.

Callie entered five minutes later. 'What are you doing, hiding in here?'

'I'm not hiding.'

'Yes you are. You're not still smarting over Tashelle dumping you, are you?'

'I'm most certainly not. That guy she went off with, Billy or whatever he was called, is welcome to her. She is way too needy.' What he didn't add was that she'd split up with the guy and was after a reconciliation.

'I thought you were quite smitten by her.'

'I was quite taken by her, but never smitten.'

'Must be hard though, working with her all day at the university.'

'I don't see too much of her, luckily.'

'Looks like Daisy might be making it

up with her ex.' She looked out of the door at them in the dining room, getting food. 'I love a happy ending.'

So did he. It just wasn't his turn.

★   ★   ★

The hour hand had passed eleven when Daisy looked at the clock. She and Matt were standing to one side of the living room, watching the others dancing. She longed to join them, but the only dancing Matt ever did was to the slow numbers. His arm was around her shoulders, clinging on.

She hadn't seen Seth for a while now, wondering if he'd gone to bed — but he was due to sleep on the sofa bed in this room, so it was unlikely. Perhaps he'd gone off outside with that woman he was dancing with earlier? No, she was on a sofa nearby, talking to Callie.

'I bet you'll be glad to get back to the peace and quiet of your parents' house,' Matt shouted above the music, pulling her in even closer. 'We'll travel first thing in the morning. I guess your companions won't mind me putting my head down on a sofa. If this party ever finishes. You can pack a few bits tomorrow and we'll arrange to pick up your other things after Christmas.'

What used to be a sense of security, of safety, of love, suddenly felt like a prison. She broke out in goose bumps. They wanted different things, her and Matt. He needed a little woman he could dominate, and she was not that person any more.

She freed herself from his embrace, indicated a route through the crowd and went on ahead, assuming he was following. She led him out into the hall, standing by the stairs until he caught up.

'That's better, some time alone.' He went to put his arm round her, but she side-stepped him.

'Matt, I'm not going anywhere with you.'

'You'd rather catch the train back?'

'No. I've already made plans for Christmas. Our relationship, as girlfriend and boyfriend, is already finished.'

'It was, but I forgive you, so it's all OK now.'

She stepped backwards. 'No, you're not listening. I don't want to be your girlfriend.'

'Then we'll get married.'

Daisy turned in a circle, clutching her head, not knowing what else to do with her frustration!

'I'm sorry, Matt. I don't love you. I don't want to be with you. End of.'

'But what will I do over the holidays without a girlfriend?'

Her frustration turned to irritation. 'That's a perfect example of why I don't want to get back with you. You're so self-centred. It's always, *how does it affect you?* You never think of me.'

'But I've offered to pay for things.'

'So you can have them your way. Take this dress. I got compliments from other people. Not from you, though. Oh, that's enough. I didn't want it to end like this, but I didn't ask you to come here, Matt. You just did what *you* wanted to, as you always do.'

The door into the dining room opened. Toby peered out with Bea.

'Is everything all right here?' said Toby.

Had she shouted so loudly that they'd heard her in there? She was mortified. She'd hoped to do this all quietly and tastefully. Trust her!

'Yes, we're fine, thank you. Matt and I have said what we needed to say to each other and he's just leaving.'

'But I — ' Matt started.

'Aren't you, Matt.' She made sure it was a statement, not a question.

'I suppose I am.' He looked at Toby and Bea, then back at her. 'Lucky for you I've only had orange juice and I can drive.'

He strode to the door, stopping to pick up his coat and scarf. He turned back to face Daisy.

'You know where I am when you change your mind.' With that he yanked open the door, not quite slamming it behind him.

'You OK?' said Bea, coming closer

and placing a hand on her arm.

'Never better, Bea.' So much better, she wanted to sing out at the sense of freedom. 'Just give me a moment to get my breath back, and I'll rejoin the party.'

Bea tapped her forearm twice and she and Toby left her alone.

* * *

Back in the living room, it was like nothing had happened, as if Matt had never been there — or would have been if her heart hadn't been pounding at a rate of knots.

Calm down, it's done. For now.

No doubt he'd go scurrying back to his parents and hers, saying how unreasonable she'd been. It's what he'd done when she'd applied for uni. On that occasion it had done him no good as both sets of parents had supported her decision.

She looked around for Seth, not at all sure if she'd approach him even if he were here. She still couldn't locate him. Perhaps he'd found another new woman, one of Callie's many sophisticated acquaintances.

Her heart had slowed to a normal pace now and she breathed out a sigh, only to jump when a hand landed on her shoulder. For a split second she thought Matt was back. She couldn't describe the relief when she saw Seth standing there.

'I'm sorry, Daisy. Bea just told me that Matt's gone,' he said.

'Yes, because I told him to go.'

'Are you all right?'

She wished people would stop asking her that. The answer was far from simple. Without much conscious thought on her part, she said, 'I'm fine. Can we dance, please?'

He looked taken aback, but nevertheless replied, 'Of course we can.'

He indicated she should go ahead and followed her into the dining room, in time for the first few bars of *Last Christmas. How appropriate*, she thought.

Last Christmas she was with Matt. This Christmas she wouldn't be. Had she given her heart to him? She wasn't sure she ever truly had.

Seth placed his hands lightly round her waist as she placed hers on his shoulders. How different to Matt, who grasped her so forcefully at times that he hurt her.

After a few seconds, he asked, 'So, am I allowed to ask what happened?'

'You are nosy, aren't you?' she replied, wishing at the same time she could spill the whole sorry story to him. Was it wise?

'Yes, I am. It's what makes me good at my job, always asking questions.'

'If you must know, I've gone and done it.'

'Uh, what exactly? Robbed a bank?'

She giggled. 'No! I've brought my relationship with Matt to a proper close. It only slowly faded away over the last summer holiday, but it was all a bit woolly really.'

'And you're happy with that?'

'Ecstatic,' she admitted. 'It's a release and now I can properly move forward. The brooding presence of my broken relationship was holding me back before.'

'Very poetic. So, what comes next?'

She thought for a while. 'Apart from finishing the biology degree? I don't know. But I'll have fun finding out.'

Being so close to him gave her a hope that she'd find out with him. Not very likely, with him being up in Northumberland. A hot flush came over her, causing her to pull back a little from Seth and fan her face.

'It is a bit warm in here now,' said Seth. 'Shall we get some air?'

She nodded. They went round the dancers and through the patio door onto the decking. Conscious that they'd be seen from the room, she carried on round to a small paved area hidden from the partygoers.

'It's lovely and cool out here.' She looked up at the clear sky, the stars faint because of the full moon. 'Isn't that wonderful? It never fails to amaze me.'

Seth stood close to her. 'Simple pleasures. When I'm somewhere, doing a dig, camping where there's no light pollution and no moon, I love to lie on the ground to look up at the stars. Especially in shooting star season.'

'Sounds great.'

'Have you never done that?'

She looked at him, bathed in the glow of the moon, his features sharp with the light and shadow. 'Never. But I'd like to.'

She pictured herself next to him on damp grass, holding hands, looking up. They were alone in the fantasy, lying there all night in each other's arms.

She shivered. He put his arm around her.

'The air's cooling for a while, but you've got to remember it's midwinter.'

'Brrr, you're not joking.' She huddled into him and he pulled her in closer, placing both arms round her. 'You're nice and warm.'

'I've got shirt sleeves, you've only got straps.'

'I'm sorry. I hope you don't think I led you out here for an ulterior motive.' She wanted to politely remove herself from his arms, but she couldn't make herself do it.

'Of course I don't think that. I'm quite happy to go where you lead.' When she frowned he added, 'Too cheesy?'

'A little, but I don't mind cheesy.'

They laughed as they got closer, his face only centimetres from hers, looking down into her face. His green eyes were now dark, unreadable. His lips did all the talking as they met hers, warm, soft. When he went to pull away she kept hold of him, wanting the new sensations inside her to last a little longer.

When they finally drew apart, he said, 'Shall we go back into the warm?'

'It'd be nice to stay out here a little longer.'

She hoped she'd conveyed her wish

to kiss him once again. He got the message loud and clear and they went in for round two.

4

Daisy woke early, before any daylight had invaded her room.

The first thing she remembered was Matt. A brief panic washed over her when she became convinced she'd gone home with him and was waking up in her own bed. It took a few seconds to realise that wasn't the case. She remembered now: that's what she'd been dreaming about.

Her mind searched for a while for what had really happened.

Seth. She'd spent the rest of the evening, after Matt had gone, dancing with him and kissing him, until one o'clock in the morning, when the last of the guests had departed.

She'd wondered briefly if Seth would suggest sharing her bed, but no — and really she was quite glad. Whatever mad sensations had taken over her body and

51

brain — and she had to admit they were really rather lovely sensations — she didn't want to completely lose her mind.

He'd instead pulled out the sofa bed as planned, and had been unrolling his sleeping bag as Daisy had wished him goodnight. With others in the room, she hadn't kissed him. His cheeky half smile had been recompense enough.

She savoured the wobbly feeling deep inside her. He was going to be there over Christmas. There'd be plenty of time to get to know him.

With that she dozed, until she heard voices and the bathroom door click shut. She sat up and looked at the clock: quarter to seven. Really? She thumped back on the. pillow briefly but soon sat up again. She might as well get up.

Pulling on her dressing gown, she yawned, shuffled towards the door and headed out onto the landing. Below, someone seemed to be speaking on a phone. It was Seth. She didn't want her greeting to be a simple wave as she passed, so she decided to wait until he'd finished. Perhaps she'd go into the bathroom when whoever was in there came out.

She didn't mean to overhear the conversation, but, apart from putting her fingers in her ears, it was inevitable.

'Yeah yeah,' came Seth's voice, impatient. 'I get that. I know, I said I would and I will. It's just — now, today?' There was a pause before he said, 'Of course. No, I realise that, Henry. It's now or never . . . She can't? So you're already shorthanded. OK, OK, I'll get my backside up there somehow. I guess I need to get a train to Alnmouth . . . Yeah. That's handy. It'll be expensive at this short notice . . . I see . . . yep . . . got it. I'll let you know my arrival time after I look it up. Bye.'

The telephone call had apparently come to an end. Daisy didn't wait to hear if Seth would make any more calls, instead running back to her bedroom and clicking the door shut. She opened the wardrobe, shuffling through her clothes, cursing her stupidity. Did she really think a man like that would stick around? An interesting man who made her laugh, who made her feel she could do anything?

Finally settling on a pair of jeans and a long sleeved t-shirt, she pulled them on quickly, almost falling over as she got tangled in the legs. Sitting down to pull on some socks, she rested her head on her knees. Regret and recriminations filled her head. Really, if she'd just been more remarkable, Seth might have stuck around.

Who was this Henry? Short for Henrietta? Some tall, willowy blonde with a PhD in astrophysics, able to play the piano superbly who wowed all she met with her witty repartee? She chuckled. That was absurd even for her. Honestly, why did she have this hang-up about being boring?

Because Matt had made her feel like that, the small town girl on his arm, to be put down in the most affectionate way. Still she couldn't shake off the idea that she'd amount to nothing without him and never do anything outside the box.

She got up, shaking the thoughts from her. She hadn't even met Seth this time two days ago. It should be easy to let him go.

* * *

Seth's heart lifted, then immediately sank, when Daisy strolled nonchalantly into the dining room. She greeted everyone at the table with a half-hearted smile as they sat with bowls of cereal and mugs of tea. Was she regretting spending time with him at the party?

'So what's the rush?' Dave said to Seth.

'Seth's got to leave in a hurry,' Callie explained to Daisy. 'He's just telling us why.'

'Oh, has he?' Daisy said in a light tone. She seemed disinterested as she stood with her arms crossed.

'There's this site, see, a dig . . . ' he started, wanting her to understand why he was leaving when they'd only just met. Even if it turned out she wasn't bothered. 'Henry, my department head, has wanted to get back to it for donkey's years. He worked on it as a young archaeologist. But the owner, James MacKinnon, closed it prematurely about thirty years back and hasn't allowed anyone near it since, despite several requests.'

'Where did you say you had to go?' Bea asked.

'A place called Sealfarne Island. It's one of the Farne Islands, off the Northumberland coast.'

'Near Lindisfarne, Holy Island,' said Daisy when Bea looked confused. 'It's an odd time of year to be doing a dig,' she added, almost accusingly.

'Well, yes, it is. But Sir James is away until the New Year and his son, Angus, is keen to get us on there. I'm not sure how much we can do in the time, but Henry's waited many years and I feel I can't let him down.'

'If you've gotta go, you've gotta go,' said Daisy, heading to the kitchen.

Could it be she was upset he was going, rather than indifferent to him? He'd never been good at romance signals. He'd thought that Tashelle cared about him, but look what happened there.

'So,' Seth continued, holding up his phone, 'I've just looked up the trains from Kings Cross, and I'm going to book the one leaving at nine-thirty. Providing there are seats.'

Daisy returned with a glass of orange juice, sitting opposite him.

'I hope you don't mind too much.' Seth looked round at his friends, his eyes coming to rest on her. Her finger was tracing the pattern on the table mat and she didn't look at him. 'I'd better go and get sorted.'

He left them, going to the living room to pack up his things. Good job they'd organised everything from the department as he didn't have time even to go back to his flat in Berwick.

Daisy walked in as he was rolling the

57

sleeping bag up, her smile more endearing now.

'Would you like some food for your journey?'

'A sandwich might be a good idea.'

She nodded and made to turn away. He strode over to her, taking hold of her arm before she'd started walking.

'I'm sorry about how this looks, Daisy. I honestly was intending to stay for Christmas. I was very keen to get to know you better. I'm not sure whether you simply don't care, or if you're cross with me.'

After some moments thought, she said, 'I'm disappointed, Seth. I felt we connected, and I was looking forward to you staying. You know, I'm not really a one-night stand kinda gal.' She followed it quickly with, 'Even when it's an innocent night.'

'Neither am I, despite what it looks like.'

'I hope you have a good Christmas there, on Sealfarne. I visited the Farnes once, on a boat trip, just going round them, basically. They're rather lovely in summer, though this time of year . . . '

'Tell me about it! Tents in December in the middle of nowhere, but . . . We might turn up something that makes it worthwhile, but it won't be as good as being here — with you.'

She looked down, tucking a tendril of hair behind her ear.

A mad idea popped into his head. Impractical, surely. Potty, without doubt.

'Why don't you come with me? You won't need to pay your train fare — and you said you were looking to reinvent yourself.'

Her head went up, her eyes widening. 'When did I say that?'

'In the wee small hours, after a few beers.'

'Yes, well. It's amazing the confidence an alcohol jacket gives you.'

'I'm serious, Daisy. The student who initially said she'd go with Henry's team has dropped out. They're set up for six people. You'd be useful.'

'I'm no archaeologist.'

'Neither are a lot of the people who help out. We get all sorts, including students like yourself.'

'I don't think so. It's probably best we say our goodbyes now.'

* * *

Daisy savoured the long kiss with Seth. She could feel the tears swelling behind her eyes. No, she wouldn't cry. Not in front of him. This might be the last time she saw him, with them being over three hundred miles apart. She couldn't quite believe it was the end when there'd barely been a beginning, but there it was.

She pulled away first, rushing to the dining room door for a quick escape to her bedroom.

'Daisy, please?'

His quiet, determined voice halted her in her steps. Twisting back she saw the sadness. What was the point?

Then it was if something snapped in her head.

Why not go? Why not experience something completely new? Do something mad!

'Yes, I will come,' she said so abruptly that he jumped — then they both laughed with relief.

'You won't regret it,' said Seth, his green eyes alight with mischief.

'I think I already am,' she giggled.

After that there was a flurry of activity as they told the others and Daisy realised just how unprepared she was for the whole thing.

'What about boots? And a waterproof, warm jacket?' suggested Dave.

'I don't have any,' Daisy admitted.

'I do!' said Callie, who was the same size.

In fact, Callie had everything she needed, from her expeditions abroad. Daisy packed her other items while Seth booked the trains. It was barely an hour later that she was in the hall with a rucksack, looking like a seasoned hiker.

She took a deep breath in, blowing it out slowly as she closed her eyes. This

61

might well turn out to be a one-trip fling of madness. It might also have to carry her through the rest of her humdrum life.

* ★ ★

The train pulled in to Alnmouth station just after one in the afternoon. The station was much smaller than Daisy had imagined, and seemed to be in the middle of nowhere. Seth was the first to get up, fetching her rucksack first before he went back for his.

'Ready?' he asked, as they waited for the doors to open.

'Ready as I'll ever be.'

'Henry should be here by now.'

Sure enough, there was a middle-aged man with a rug of greying hair that looked as if it needed a cut. He had a large rucksack balanced on his back as he stood on the platform looking off into the distance.

'Henry!' Seth called. When they caught him up, he said, 'This is Daisy Morgan,

62

the student I've found to replace Amy. Daisy, this is Professor Henry Webb, my department head.'

'Pleased to meet you, Daisy,' said Henry. 'And please, we're on first name terms only. None of this 'Professor Webb' nonsense.'

They shook hands. His manner put Daisy completely at ease, relieving the knot that had formed in her stomach.

'I'm trusting that they'll be all set up by the time we reach there. I can't get hold of them so I reckon there's no signal. They were taking the trailer over on the boat with the tents and everything. Angus MacKinnon picked them up with his Jeep and they've already started digging the trenches. Or re-digging them.'

Henry's sigh was long and heartfelt.

'How are we getting to the island?' Daisy asked, realising they weren't yet by the sea.

'I've booked a taxi to take us to Seahouses,' said Henry. 'And chartered the boat to take us over to Sealfarne from there. Don't look so scared, m'dear. The wind is calm so I'm sure the trip over in the boat will be trouble free.'

She hadn't been worrying about that. But now she would.

During the taxi journey, Seth asked, 'Where has Sir James gone?'

'To Edinburgh, with Lady MacKinnon.'

There was something about the way he said the woman's name. Daisy couldn't quite put her finger on it, whether it was wistful or condemning. In all likelihood it was neither, just her vivid imagination taking over as always.

* * *

The sea was grey, reflecting the slate sky, as Sealfarne appeared on the horizon. Birds Daisy couldn't identify were flying overhead. She peered out to sea, narrowing her eyes for a better look.

'Are those seals?'

Seth moved right up close to her, trying to see where she was looking.

'They are. There'll be a lot here at the moment, with their seal pups.'

'In the winter?'

He nodded.

The island, which was the furthest out in the Farnes, loomed closer. There were low lying, sheer cliffs on two sides as they made their way round. After a second corner, there was a view of rocks and scrubby vegetation. The only building visible — tall, rectangular and made of stone — was close to the shore. It was a large house with white framed windows stuck willy-nilly in the stone-work. The only trees she could make out were gathered around it.

'How big is the island?' Daisy asked.

'About a mile by three-quarters of a mile,' Henry replied without having to think about it.

'Are there other houses, a village?'

Henry looked at Seth. 'You haven't explained?'

'I did say it was in the middle of nowhere,' said Seth. 'I guess I didn't go into detail.'

'Sealfarne Castle, as it's grandly referred to, is the only house on the island,' Henry explained. 'Sir James MacKinnon is somewhat of a recluse. His son, Angus lives on the mainland most of the time — Newcastle, I believe. He's visiting now, with James away, which is why we have such a narrow window of opportunity.'

'Seth tells me you haven't been here in thirty years,' she said.

'That's right.' Henry moved away to the other side of the boat, saying no more.

They pulled up by a small, stone jetty on the north-east side of the island, leading to a rock path and a tiny beach.

Seth helped her out of the boat and they walked up the path, towards the petite castle. Now she was closer she reckoned it had three storeys, though it was hard to tell with the odd distribution of windows. A chilly wind blew, even on land. There were no people, no village, therefore no shops. She looked over at Seth. Was he worth the discomfort? Yes, oh yes!

Standing on the path was a tall, broad man, his long, black hair blowing in the breeze. He wore a purple wool trench coat and sturdy-looking combat boots with studs.

'Welcome to Sealfarne Island,' he called, in what sounded to her like a watered down Geordie accent. His voice was deep. 'Or, welcome back, in your case, Professor Webb.'

Henry hurried up the path to shake hands with the man. He kept hold of them as he said, 'I can't thank you enough, Angus, for contacting me. My, you've grown since I last saw you.'

'I was only twelve then, Professor. Though I remember the dig vividly. It was lucky I found the letters you sent to my father over the years, requesting to come back here.'

'He never replied to any of them. I'm so glad you're sympathetic to the historical heritage of this small island.'

'It was my mother who was interested, really. Father never was.'

Henry patted the younger man's

hand. 'Yes, I realised that.'

'I have the Jeep. I'll drive you over to the camp.' Angus released his hands and strode away.

'How far is it from here?' Daisy asked.

'About three-quarters of a mile,' replied Henry. 'It's not far from the southern corner.'

The ride along the makeshift track was bumpy, making her feel far queasier than the boat had done. They drove through a slight valley, as small hillocks rose up on either side. The space was filled with low-lying, deep green plants, along with gorse bushes, some of which were in flower. The track climbed slightly up, passing a third, even smaller hillock.

'That's Stow Rise,' Henry told her. 'It's where the monks' burial ground is situated.'

Starting a slight descent, it wasn't long before they turned right on the track. By the time they pulled up near the tents, Sealfarne Castle was hidden. The camp wasn't far from the foot of Stow Rise, though Henry told her that the trench wasn't visible from there.

Six small, curved, grey tents sat in three-quarters of a circle on a piece of bare ground. In the centre there was a fire burning, around which were placed six foldable chairs.

A welcoming committee came to meet them, two women and a man.

'Rich O'Neill, at your service,' said the man in a lilting Irish accent, shaking her hand enthusiastically. A thatch of dark blond hair covered his head and chin. Daisy reckoned he was in his thirties. He peered over at Seth. 'Why, you're a dark horse, aren't you?'

'It's not like that,' Daisy piped up before she'd had time to think about it. What a daft thing to say — of course it was like that.

He held his hands up. 'It's none of my business what it's like.'

Daisy couldn't help but notice the look that passed between Seth and Rich. Eyebrows raised on Seth's part, eyes narrowed on Rich's. She wondered if she'd walked into a situation she didn't understand. These people worked together all the time. There were bound to be strains.

'Hi, I'm Freja Johansson,' said the woman with short blonde curly hair, bright blue eyes beaming at her. She had a slight accent, Scandinavian of some sort. She also shook Daisy's hand. 'I used to be an archaeologist on Henry's team, but I present TV programmes now, like *The Dig Squad* and *History in Your Garden*.'

'Oh yes, I've seen them,' said Daisy, hoping she didn't sound too fan-ish.

'And always sensationalising our profession with so-called major finds and stunts,' tutted the other woman, raven haired and black eyed with olive skin. Very pretty. 'I'm Dr Tashelle Peignton.'

She didn't shake Daisy's hand, instead going over to kiss Seth on the cheek before coming back to stand by the first tent.

Uh-oh. What was going on here? Tashelle gave Daisy the once over, and by the frown and slight curl to her lip,

70

she didn't like what she saw.

'We're all doctors,' said Rich. 'You don't have to make a big thing about it.'

Tashelle ignored him.

Seth and Henry walked over to Angus to thank him for the lift. They spoke for a while, leaving Daisy on her own, watching the others getting back to what they were doing.

'Your tent's over there,' said Tashelle, waving her hand at the fourth tent in the circle. 'Seth can go here. And I'm here.' She pointed to the first and second tents.

Convenient. Though maybe the tents had already been allocated and the fourth had been earmarked for the student who'd dropped out.

Angus drove off, leaving Seth free to join them.

'We need to get sorted. It'll be dark soon,' he said.

Daisy looked at the sky. It was hard to tell with it already being so grey, but it was looking gloomier. Everyone took her lead and looked up.

'That's the problem with digging in the northern hemisphere in the winter,' said Henry. 'Not enough daylight. Tashelle, would you show me and Seth around what you've all already done?'

'Of course,' said Tashelle. 'We've marked out three trenches in the different areas and started on the digging.'

'Man, it's times like these I realise how useful those mechanical diggers are,' said Rich.

'Not something we had the time or budget for,' Henry said with reluctant acceptance.

The wind whipped up and a darker cloud blew over from the east. A piercing scream rent the air, propelling Daisy to Seth's side. She noticed Freja had also moved closer to the group.

'It's only a fox,' said Henry.

Daisy had seen the odd urban fox in her home town, but never heard a sound as unearthly as that before. Looking around, the whole place was alien, far from home and with people she didn't know. She couldn't see past the nine days that stretched endlessly ahead. And first, she had to get through the long, long night.

5

It was dark by the time Seth, Henry and Tashelle returned, their arrival heralded by a torch beam. Rich had built a fire with wood they'd had to bring across from the mainland, the only trees being by Sealfarne Castle.

Daisy had her hands round a steaming tin mug of tea, sitting near the fire with Freja, who'd taken a shine to her. Nevertheless, she was relieved to see Seth, worried they could have fallen down a hole, or a cliff somewhere. She had no idea where the cliffs were in relation to their position.

'The wanderers return,' said Rich. 'Shame on you, Seth, for abandoning your lovely lady friend. Or friend who's a lady . . . whatever.'

'There'd have been no point in taking Daisy, Rich — think about it,' said Seth. 'Better to acquaint her with it in proper daylight.'

'If we ever get any proper daylight,' Rich muttered. He eyed up Seth in the firelight, though Seth had already moved on.

'I don't know about these two, but I'm ready for a cup of tea,' said Henry, breaking the tension. 'And some food, if there's any going.'

'Got the grub cooking in the pot,' said Rich. 'Nice lamb stew. Make the most of it. We only brought this and chicken. It'll be rabbit stew every day after that.'

Daisy laughed and knew immediately it was the wrong thing to do.

'You think he's joking?' said Tashelle, unzipping her jacket as she sat down, then taking the mug proffered by Rich. 'We're lucky to get those. They're only here because some must have jumped on a boat hundreds of years ago and got off when the boat stopped here. The monks used to eat them. I presume you know about the monks.' It was a dismissive statement, one that implied she probably knew nothing at all.

'Yes, Seth told me on the train about the seventh century monastery and the possibility of a Bronze Age settlement.'

'No possibility about it, m'dear,' said Henry, joining them. 'We definitely found evidence, albeit slight, when I was here last time. Trouble is, we were forced to leave it here.' He shook his head and added no more.

'At least the temperature's mild — for the time of year, that is,' said Tashelle. 'I've no idea how we could even have attempted anything if the ground had been frozen.'

'True,' said Henry. 'But I would have found some way. Too good an opportunity to pass up.'

'Is it a very important site?' Daisy hoped it wasn't a silly question.

'We won't know until we do more digging,' Henry explained. 'It was certainly shaping up to be interesting. It was quite a surprise to find Bronze Age items here.'

'What did you expect to find, initially?'

'Just evidence of the monastery.'

'We have three trenches open,' Seth said, standing behind Daisy. 'Trench 1 is the Bronze Age site, Trench 2 is where the monastery sat, and Trench 3 is the monks' burial ground at the start of Stow Rise. I'll take you to Trench 1 with me tomorrow, show you the ropes.'

Daisy could see how passionate Seth was about his job and felt his enthusiasm infect her. She couldn't wait to get started, despite all the inconveniences ahead and simmering tensions.

'Grub's up,' said Rich, stirring the pot. 'Get it while it's hot.' He served it into bowls and passed them around.

By the time Seth had collected his supper, Henry had already sat next to Daisy. With Freja on the other side, she was disappointed when Seth had to sit further away. Tashelle was the last to sit down, placing herself next to Seth — and close at that. A niggle of envy ran through Daisy. Still, there'd be plenty of other times to get close to him.

Despite Henry and Freja talking to each other either side of her, Daisy was able to make out Tashelle saying, 'I've missed you, Seth, while you've been in Crete.'

'I've only been gone three weeks.'

'Did you get my texts?'

'You know I did. I answered them.'

'Not all of them.'

'I think you know — '

'Is the stew OK?' Rich interrupted, making Daisy miss the rest of Seth's reply. Really, she shouldn't have been listening in the first place.

There were various positive responses, including from Daisy who was enjoying the food. With the tents set up round the fire, the first part of the night should at least be fairly comfortable.

After the meal, there was a discussion about how they'd proceed the next day. Henry told them of his previous finds, expressing the hope that the mechanical digger Sir James had hired to cover the sites had not done too much damage.

'I only hope we're able to locate everything we had before. Not that any of it will be in its original place.' He lowered his head.

The next hour or so was filled with Henry telling them what he could remember of the first dig and giving out copies of the original reports. They examined them with torches but Daisy found it hard to make head or tail of it all. After that, Seth told them how he'd fared in Crete. The rest of the evening was filled with general chit-chat.

Around nine-thirty, Henry straightened himself with purpose, declaring, 'I think we should turn in early tonight. I suggest we're all up at seven, to give us time for breakfast before starting at eight. It'll be getting light by then, although sunrise isn't until eight-thirty.'

Of course, it had got dark earlier than in London, and it would get light later, Daisy realised. She felt a small tremor of panic as the darkness began to feel like a prison closing around her.

Everyone rose, wishing each other good night. Seth headed towards Daisy, about to say something when Tashelle stepped between them, facing her.

'Your tent's over there, remember?' she said, like a teacher telling a student off.

'Yes, I do remember. Goodnight Seth.'

'Goodnight,' he replied, his eyes dark in the firelight.

They hesitated a moment before each went to their own tent.

★   ★   ★

By seven-thirty the next morning, the whole group, apart from Freja, were sitting round the fire eating porridge. Rich had been up since six-thirty, getting the fire ready in the torchlight.

'We'd better call Freja again,' said Henry, sitting on the opposite side of the fire from Daisy.

'I've called her twice already,' Tashelle growled. 'She hasn't changed from when she was in the department. Always the last to get her lazy rear out of bed. Heaven only knows how she copes on location with a TV crew.'

Seth chuckled. 'Hotels, is the answer. I doubt very much that they sleep on site.'

'She never was cut out for this game. She was so disorganised. Her record keeping was appalling. Really, I've no idea how she got picked up by a TV company.'

'Personality, darling!' a voice called out from the darkness. Freja appeared, ghostlike, in a long white kaftan. 'You need that for TV. No point being a miserable academic and nothing else.'

Tashelle didn't reply, simply taking another spoonful of porridge.

For several minutes people concentrated on eating while Daisy's mind wandered. At home, Mum would be getting the bulk of the festive food today. She'd start making the desserts and pastries. Daisy would miss the food, the games, the warmth of family, especially when Granny Evans came around. But she would have missed it anyway, staying in London.

She'd have to content herself with looking forward to seeing her family at

New Year. Matt was going on a skiing break then, as he'd informed her at the party. He'd even suggested he might be able to get her a last minute booking. But skiing had never interested her in the way it did Matt. She was picturing decorating the family tree when she felt someone sit next to her.

Seth. He smiled warmly and she reciprocated. He'd been commandeered by Tashelle when they'd first gathered, but she was now in conversation with Henry.

'You looked miles away,' said Seth.

'Just thinking about Mum and Dad. They seemed quite shocked when I rang them to say they might not be able to reach me by phone because I was coming here.'

'Any regrets about not going back with Matt?'

She hesitated. His brow puckered. 'No way.'

His face relaxed. She wanted to ask what the deal was with Tashelle, but now wasn't the time with everyone around.

Tashelle came up behind them, as if summoned by Daisy's thoughts.

'I'm claiming Daisy to assist me in Trench 3.'

Daisy's heart sank. A day of snarkiness she could do without.

'Sorry — I claimed her last night, if you recall,' said Seth.

'You said she was a biology student, and there were skeletal remains of the monks in Trench 3,' Tashelle countered. 'I'm sure Henry will agree.'

Henry looked up from his porridge, his eyes swinging from one to the other.

'Well, out of the five of us, Seth will initially be alone in Trench 1, so maybe it's better if Daisy goes there. She can be his assistant.'

'If Seth needs help, I'll go to Trench 1 and Daisy can help Rich in Trench 3.'

'But you're more an expert on human remains,' said Seth.

Daisy didn't like being the cause of any bad feeling between them, though she had already fallen foul of Tashelle, she knew.

'I agree,' Henry said, his voice oozing authority. 'Daisy will go with Seth for now.'

'Right,' said Tashelle, marching to her tent.

'Just what we need,' said Freja. 'Madame Peignton in a bad mood.'

'And you'd better get yourself ready, sharpish,' Henry said, turning to Freja. 'It's starting to get light already and we'll be setting off very soon.'

Daisy looked at the eastern horizon, towards where the Bronze Age site at Trench 1 was apparently situated. Sure enough, the first band of pale misty light was pushing against the darkness.

She only hoped she would be a help to Seth, not be a hindrance, and that she'd pick up whatever he taught her quickly and he wouldn't be sorry he'd brought her here.

6

Daisy had proved a good pupil so far, listening carefully to Seth's instructions about scraping the soil towards her with the edge of the trowel to reveal what was beneath. She was hunkering down, working on the area Seth had given her, her tongue poking out in concentration.

So far, so good. But he'd seen even the most enthusiastic of students tire quite quickly of the painstaking task. If he'd wanted to stay in contact it might have been better to arrange to see her in the New Year — except she was heading home to see her parents then. After that, he'd be back to his university in Berwick and she'd be back at hers in London. Maintaining any kind of relationship would be difficult.

'Have you detected anything different yet?' he called across from a few feet away.

'Not a sausage. It's all the same soil, not even any colour difference.'

'Same here. I'm beginning to wonder if James MacKinnon didn't just tip out the artefacts and cover them, but dug a hole to bury them deeper.'

A weak sun had now escaped through the clouds to light the area up a little better than when they'd first arrived. Seth was thankful for small mercies.

'Oh, hang on, what's this?' He felt his heart speed up as he detected a change in soil colour.

Daisy left her patch and headed over, her face eager. 'What have you found?'

He lifted up a brown stone. 'Zilch. Never mind. Early days.'

'Shame,' said Daisy, returning to her spot.

'Hi there, how's it going?'

Seth and Daisy twirled round to see Angus. He was wearing the same coat and boots, but this time his hair was tied back and he was holding a walking stick with a puffin carved into the top.

'Nothing as yet,' Seth replied. 'We've only been at it less than four hours though.'

'I thought something might be uncovered quickly as it had simply been covered over. The other two trenches haven't had much luck either.'

Seth stood and walked towards Angus.

'Do you know for certain your father left the artefacts there? Might he have removed them and put them elsewhere, thrown them away, or even sent them to a museum?'

'No, I'm pretty sure he simply covered them over. I remember the day the mini digger arrived on the boat and my father saying something along the lines of burying the past and letting it all rest in peace.'

'That's an odd thing to say.' Daisy sat on the vegetation next to where she'd been digging.

'It is, isn't it? I remember being very disappointed, fascinated as I was by the possibility of a Bronze Age settlement. I knew there'd been Vikings later and that they sacked the monastery here, as they did at Lindisfarne.'

Angus's face was lit by a smile. It was the first time he'd looked anything but deadly serious.

'My mother used to bring me to this trench, and the other two. But it was this one we were both most interested in. It was she who encouraged my father to let the archaeologists investigate. He had no interest. Mary Armstrong was my live-in tutor at the time. She didn't approve of the dig and discouraged me from going. She'd get quite cross when my mother took me regardless.

'I remember Henry. Always a jolly man, much younger then, of course. He and my mother would chat for ages about the possibilities of the finds.'

'Why did your father decide to bring it to an end?' Daisy asked.

Angus's smile disappeared. He pulled his arms in tight to his body, as if he trying to shrink away.

'I — I can't say. My mother and he had argued about it quite a bit while it was happening. Lack of privacy maybe, which he values above all else. In the end, of course, he got his way . . . I should go, leave you to get on.'

Seth wiped his hand on his already dirty jeans. 'Will you get into trouble when your father finds out? It'll be obvious we've been here, even if we put all the soil back.'

Angus laughed, but it was mirthless. 'I wasn't quite big enough to handle myself with him back then, but I am now.'

Seth had no doubt this was true, with the height and breadth of him.

'But anyway, my father is my problem, so don't go troubling yourself about it.' He lifted his hand in the air in farewell and was soon striding across the vegetation.

Seth watched him as he went. *Why now?* It was a question he'd asked himself several times. Sir James must have left the island on a number of occasions in the last thirty years. Why had Angus left it this long?

Daisy walked around the trench to Seth. 'He seemed quite anxious, don't you think?'

'Yep, just a little. But then, so would I be if I'd gone behind my father's back to do something I knew he wouldn't like, despite what he says.' Seth pulled his mobile out of his jacket pocket to check the time. 'It'll be lunch soon. Let's get a bit more done. I'd like to take some good news back to the camp if possible.'

Daisy saluted him. 'Aye aye, captain.'

'I think you'll find that Henry's very much the captain. I'm still way down the pecking order. More of a lieutenant. Though don't say that in Rich's hearing.'

'Why's that?'

'I got the promotion in the summer to senior lecturer that Rich was after. I thought he'd get it, to be honest, since he's been in the department longer than me, and he's older. But Henry and the rest of the interviewing committee decided to give it to me.' He shrugged.

'That explains the bad vibes I've

been picking up between you two.'

'I feel terrible, but at the same time, I've got to think of my career.'

Daisy was too close for him to resist taking hold of her arm and drawing her closer. She beamed at him and he knew she was quite happy with what it was obvious he was about to do. Sure enough, she responded eagerly to his kisses.

Apart again, Daisy said, 'What about Tashelle? She's been rather . . . shall we say, possessive?'

'Uh, well. I should have told you before. Long story short, we were an item for a while. She went off with someone else, better off, a minor celebrity. When her new boyfriend did the same to her, she wanted to get back with me.'

'And still does by the looks of it. That explains a lot. We should be careful when she's around.'

'Why should we? She dumped me. I'm not hiding away and don't you feel you should. OK?'

'You're right, I guess.'

'Right, let's get digging!'

Tashelle had made her own bed and she'd have to learn to lie in it alone. She was known for getting moody when she couldn't get her own way. He only hoped Henry would sort her out if she tried anything.

★ ★ ★

It had been Tashelle's turn to prepare lunch, so she'd made them all cheese salad sandwiches. Daisy reckoned she'd got the leftover crumbs of the cheese, and the limpest part of the lettuce, but she didn't complain. She didn't want to get any more on the bad side of Tashelle than she had to. At least the cakes Freja had brought over from the mainland had filled the hole left. And her back was getting a rest.

There'd been an air of dejection among the group, due to no one making any finds. Henry particularly, mentioning several times how few days they had left, had taken it badly.

It was a relief to be back to at Trench

92

1, even though she was bending over again at an awkward angle. Seth, back in his space, was singing to himself, though she couldn't quite work out what.

'Strange to think it's Christmas Day after tomorrow,' he called across. 'I guess my folks will be sunning themselves in Sidney, or Canberra, or wherever they are. They're not good at keeping me abreast of such things.'

'I was thinking the same — about Christmas, that is, not your parents,' she laughed. 'Callie and the others will be — hold on, what's this?' She scraped the trowel a few times over the area she'd been working. It could just be a different type of soil, or a piece of rock. There was only a slight difference in colour to the soil. No, there was a definite curve.

Seth was already by her side when she stopped scraping. 'Let me have a look,' he said, hunkering down.

She moved back to let him in. He produced a small paintbrush from his back pocket before alternately scraping and brushing at the area.

She watched with fascination as the piece she'd discovered took shape. There was now an unmistakable curve, ridged rather than smooth. Seth carried on, digging the tip of his trowel in to remove some soil. It was a good job he knew what he was doing. She may well have had the item in several pieces by now.

As he gently lifted what, to her, looked like a lump of earth encrusted stone, he whistled.

'Congratulations, Daisy! Unless the others have already had some success, I think you might have found the first piece.'

'But the first piece of what?'

'A pot of some sort. I'll have to get it cleaned to get a good look, but you see these coil marks?'

She moved in for a closer look. 'I think so.'

'It's Bronze Age, I'd say. Now we've found this, if we concentrate on your end, we may well turn up more. Except . . . '

She knew it was too good to be true. 'Except?'

94

'If Sir James just tipped the finds in, they could be anywhere. They might even be in the wrong trenches.'

'Oh boy.'

Seth tipped her head up. 'Don't look so down. We'll dig close together. I'll sure we'll find more now. And there are also the items that never got dug up. They'll still be in the same place.' He leant forward and pecked her mouth. 'Well done. Perhaps you'll be my good luck charm.'

She kissed him back. 'I'll do my best.'

★ ★ ★

Around the camp fire that evening, Tashelle was not in a good mood.

'Beginner's luck,' she said, for the second time, of Daisy's find, which had turned out to be the first item located. 'Good job Seth was there, otherwise she'd probably have ruined it.'

'Absolutely,' said Daisy. 'I wouldn't have liked to have tried to dig it out. Seth was brilliant.' She hoped by agreeing with Tashelle that she'd do some damage limitation. 'And it's great that you found some pieces too.'

'Why, thank you, boss!' Tashelle retorted. 'I'm so glad you approve.'

Seth murmured, 'Tashelle, give it a rest.'

She squeezed her lips in as her eyes bulged with fury. Seth had not been the best person to deliver this rebuke.

'We've all done well today, finding items in all the trenches, eventually.' Henry's face lit up with victory. 'Lots of nice pottery pieces from Trench 1. Trench 2 revealed some domestic pieces from the monastery, and they found a midden which included lots of seashells — probably the monk's staple diet. Trench 3 turned up what are probably monks' bones, though sadly in disarray. Most of the items are certainly those we recorded on the last dig. So we all deserve a pat on the back.'

Daisy hoped that would cheer Tashelle up.

Rich lifted a bottle of red wine.

'Hear, hear! Though of course, we do also have a tradition of raising a glass to the first person to make a find.'

One step forward, two steps back, thought Daisy. Nevertheless, Tashelle joined them all as they held out their tin mugs for Rich to fill. Henry made a toast and the rest of the group lifted their mugs to shout, 'To Daisy' — except Tashelle who merely took a swig of the wine.

Seth, already standing next to Daisy, sat beside her as Freja dished up the chicken stew she'd put together that evening.

'Do you ever cook on a dig, as you're so good?' Daisy said to Seth once they had their food.

'Most certainly. It's my turn tomorrow.' He half smiled and lifted his eyebrows twice.

'I'm not sure I like the way you said that.'

'You wait and see.'

★ ★ ★

Back at Trench 1 the following day after lunch, Daisy and Seth were hoping to turn up some new pieces. The ones they'd already found were in a box, numbered and tentatively matched up with the list. They'd been lucky that so many photographs had been taken at the original dig, though some of the items were damaged.

Daisy, with one earphone from her mobile stuck in her ear so she could still hear Seth if he said something, hummed along to Christmas tunes she'd downloaded. Christmas Eve. It didn't feel like it at all.

'And what were you doing this time last Christmas?' Seth called over.

She thought the question was a bit out of nowhere, until she realised she was humming *Last Christmas*.

'Helping Mum get ready.' And doing the Christingle service with Matt. He had said something along the lines of how maybe they'd bring their own children here one day. But she didn't want to think about that, let alone say it to Seth. 'What about you?'

His eyes raised heavenward and Daisy had the impression he wished he'd never brought the subject up. 'Last minute shopping with Tashelle, if you must know, before she went home to her folks in Lincoln. My parents were away then too, so I spent Christmas with my sister and her family. But she's spending it with her in-laws this year.'

'When did you split up with Tashelle?'

'When she dumped me for an old flame she met up with in Lincoln. January.' His voice lowered. 'Oh, talk of the devil. What is it with her today? That's the second time she's been over.'

'Hi,' Tashelle said in a light tone, almost like a child. 'Just seeing how you're getting on.'

Seth straightened up. 'So you said the other time. Haven't you got enough to do in your own trench? It must take you ten minutes to walk here and back.'

'I need to stretch my legs — and keep up with what's going on.'

'That's Henry's job.'

Tashelle ignored this. 'How is our new helper getting on?'

What, she couldn't bring herself to use her name now? Seth thought, saying, 'Daisy's getting on very well. She's a quick learner.'

'Well, I shall love you and leave you then.'

'Yep, you're good at that,' said Seth.

Tashelle stormed off in a huff.

'Sorry, I shouldn't have risen to it,' Seth said when the other woman was out of hearing range. 'She seems determined to get on my nerves.'

'I don't blame you for reacting.'

Seth jumped up. 'Ah, here's my relief.'

Freja was walking towards them from the other direction, her camera slung round her neck. She was another who'd left her dig from time to time, but in her case to take photos.

'Your relief?' Daisy queried.

'All will be revealed later. Freja, would you start over that side?' He pointed to an area neither of them had worked on so far.

'Sure. Before you go, can I take a photo of you two?' Freja held her camera up. 'Kneeling together in the trench.'

Seth did as he was asked, taking his place next to Daisy. Freja took several shots before being satisfied with what she had. 'Thanks.'

'See ya later, then.' Seth hurried off in the direction of the beach, only a hundred or so metres away on the southeast side of the island.

'What's he up to?' Daisy asked Freja.

'It's his turn to make the supper, that's all I know.' She laid the camera down in a bag she'd brought and got stuck in to the area Seth had indicated. It was some minutes before she said, 'So, how did you get involved with this dig?'

Daisy told Freja something vague about Seth stopping off at the house in London, discovering the team would have one missing and inviting her along to fill the gap.

'I thought you two were an item.'

'Kind of . . . early days.'

'Right. How long have you known Seth?'

This is what Daisy was trying to avoid telling her. But she didn't want to lie. 'About four days.'

'Four days!'

'But my housemates have known him for years.' She really wasn't sure of the time scale but she didn't want the woman to think she was totally barking mad. 'They like Seth a lot so I knew it'd be OK to come here with him.'

And that at least was true.

'Yah, Seth's a good sort.'

'What about you? If you're working on these shows now, how come you're helping on this dig? It can't be very TV-worthy.'

'That's for me to work out. It might turn out to be big.'

Or you might make out it is, she thought, given what Tashelle had said. Daisy was aware some of the episodes of her shows were over the top.

'Besides,' Freja continued, 'I owe

Henry a favour. I know he's long wanted to return here, and I always said I'd come with him if he got the opportunity. And seeing as it's kind of unofficial and low on funds, I thought I'd help out.'

Daisy wasn't sure whether she meant helping out on a practical level or with money. If this dig did turn out to be a big deal, no doubt Freja would be in a good position to get it featured on her programme. If Sir James would allow it.

* * *

The clouds had cleared enough to produce a deep orange sunset. It made the hillocks of Stow Rise on the left and How Rise on the right, visible as silhouettes from their position at the Bronze Age site. Wandering back to camp near the foot of Stow Rise, Daisy and Freja spotted the unmistakable light of the fire, but there was something else.

'What has Seth been up to now?' said Freja.

'How do you know it's Seth?'

'It's the kind of thing he does — a romantic soul. Look at that, tealights round the camp. None of the other three would have done that.'

Freja quickened her step though Daisy was more cautious. The plants were getting harder to make out in the twilight and the path was narrow.

Entering the camp, it was clear there were fairy lights trailed over the fronts of the tents. Close up Daisy could see they were the battery ones they'd spotted in a shop in King's Cross station. She'd found Seth in there after she'd got them coffees, but hadn't realised he'd bought them. Freja greeted Henry, Tashelle and Rich, standing by the fire.

Seth appeared from his tent, hurrying to Daisy's side when he spotted her. He kissed her cheek. 'How'd your afternoon go?'

'More pots, and a piece of metal that Freja reckons is bronze and might be part of a bracelet.' She offered the box of artefacts for inspection.

'Hey, that's wonderful. Well done.'

'Freja found it so I can't take the credit.' She'd didn't want to draw undeserved attention to herself. 'And you? What was all the mystery?'

'I spent a fruitful half-hour gathering some goodies on the shore and then some on land.'

'For supper?'

He nodded. 'But first, we need to do some record keeping. You can help me with ours. Freja and I will tell you what to write and you can fill in the form. I'll get one of the big torches so we can see better. The firelight's not good to write by.'

Freja rolled her eyes and sighed. 'Ugh, the boring side of the job.'

'But necessary,' said Tashelle, approaching with Rich. 'You have to deal with the whole package to be good at this game.'

Freja ignored her.

★ ★ ★

105

Daisy couldn't believe the array of shell-fish Seth had managed to gather: limpets, mussels, clams, cockles and even some razor clams. He'd placed them on slabs of flat rock and baked them in the fire.

'Can you eat them in winter?' Daisy asked.

'What, you think he's after poisoning you?' said Tashelle, tutting. 'Winter's the safest time for shellfish.' If she'd added a 'Duh!' at the end, Daisy wouldn't have been surprised.

'Of course I don't think he'll poison me. I just don't know about when to eat them, or how.'

'And you a biology student.'

Daisy took a moment to compose herself, work out how best to word what she wanted to say.

'Well, I know about their physiology and life cycle, which I don't suppose you're familiar with.'

Behind her she heard Rich's deep laugh.

'At last — give her as good as you get. She can be a miserable old moo.'

'Shut up, Rich,' said Tashelle.

'Tuck in, everyone,' Seth called. 'And help yourselves to greens.'

Daisy examined the offered pan. 'Spinach?'

'Dandelion and dock leaves. They're not as big as they would be in summer, but still edible.'

She went to hand the pan back.

'Don't be a wimp.' He put some on her plate.

She bent down to smell it, puckering her nose in anticipation. 'Oh, they smell OK.'

'Of course they do. Now eat up your greens like a good girl.'

He beamed at her, making her stomach turn to jelly. She wasn't sure she could eat now, feeling all wobbly as she did — but she was starving!

The meal was delicious and more filling than she'd anticipated. She felt warm and drowsy, a combination of the busy day, success, and a homely fire. Seth was next to her, relating a funny incident on another dig, where he'd fallen down a hole with Rich and they'd had to yell for help. At the end of the anecdote he collected everyone's dishes, shoving them in a bowl of hot water.

'We'll do those later. It's Christmas Eve — time for dancing!'

'For what?' Daisy said, yawning.

He went back to his tent, coming out with a tiny speaker. He plugged his phone into it and thumbed the screen before Christmas music started playing. He placed it on the large, flat rock they were using as a table, then took hold of her hand. To the strains of *I Wish It Could Be Christmas Everyday* he swung her back and forth and twirled her around as she giggled.

'Totally lame,' said Tashelle, folding her arms.

Rich pulled Tashelle up. 'Oh come on, don't be a wet blanket all your life.'

She was slow to respond, then gave in to it, looking like the whole thing was a terrible bore.

Freja put her hand out to Henry, still seated by the fire. 'Come on, Prof, I bet you can still strut your stuff.'

'I wouldn't bank on it. Why do you think I'm retiring soon?'

'You'll never retire.' Freja beckoned to him.

'Oh, all right.' Henry made a great show of heaving himself up, although he was very fit for his age. Taking Freja's hand, then placing his other hand on her shoulder they swung back and forth to the beat.

Daisy, intrigued by Henry's statement, waited until a slower song came on and they were swaying together to ask Seth about it.

'Henry's retiring?' she said softly. 'He doesn't look old enough.'

'I know. I can't see it myself. The department is his life. He's never married, nor had a partner, as far as I know. There's something quite sad about him. I wondered if he lost someone.'

Daisy looked over at him. He seemed to be having fun now, but she knew what Seth meant. There was something melancholy about him.

She put that out of her mind. Tomorrow would be another working day as usual, despite it being Christmas Day. She'd better enjoy the evening while she could.

★　★　★

Everyone else had gone to bed, leaving Seth and Daisy alone at last in front of the dying embers of the fire. Seth had been loath to make too much fuss of Daisy, not wanting to upset Tashelle, despite their split being her fault and all of her difficult behaviour since. He'd waited all day to enfold Daisy in his arms and kiss her, and that's just what he was doing.

'That was a wonderful evening, Seth,' Daisy said when they came up for air. 'It more than made up for missing Christmas Eve at my parents'.'

'And for missing Matt?'

She pulled away a little and frowned at him. 'I have not missed Matt in the slightest. Which is a revelation to me. If someone had told me I'd feel like that back in September, I'd have said they didn't know what they were talking about.'

'Had you been going out long?'

'Since I was sixteen. About seven years . . . whoa! Saying that now makes me wonder why I wasted that much of my life on him. When I think back, he was always a control freak, always disapproving of the way I did things. Most of the time I just toed the line as it made life easier.'

'Sounds like a nightmare.'

'He more or less stopped me going to university at eighteen, because we'd be apart for long periods of time. He even moaned when I said I was staying on at school. He was two years older than me and had started his own company by then. He's made a great success of it. He assumed I'd work for him, but I went to my dad's firm instead.'

Seth shook his head. If he'd felt any guilt about being responsible for spiriting her away from Matt, he certainly didn't now. 'How did you put up with that for so long?'

'I dunno. Thought it was normal, I suppose. He wanted to look after me and keep me safe, and I guess I felt loved and cared for.'

'More like controlled.'

'I realise that now — what was that?'

'What?'

'A swishing sound.'

They were both dead still for a while, listening.

'Must be my imagination,' Daisy said when there were no more sounds.

'Could be someone going to the powder room.'

They both laughed at the name Tashelle had come up with for the portable compostable loo they'd positioned behind an eight-foot rock.

'Too much information!' Daisy looked at her watch, a present last year from Matt. 'It's nearly midnight. Shame we haven't any mistletoe.'

'Who needs mistletoe?'

They gazed at her watch as the seconds ticked away, until 00.00 appeared on the screen, then they held each other and kissed for long seconds.

'I have something for you.' Seth shuffled around in the space next to him, producing a roughly wrapped parcel, the paper recycled from the magazine he'd been reading on the train.

'You shouldn't have. I've nothing for you.'

'It doesn't matter. Go on, open it.' She unwrapped it to reveal a book on the basics of archaeology. 'It was my first book on the subject, given to me by my parents when I was eighteen. I carry it everywhere. It's time to give it to someone else it might be useful to.'

She looked both touched and worried.

'Are you sure? Isn't it precious?'

'It is. That's why I've given it to you.'

'Oh Seth . . .'

'We'd better head to bed, otherwise we'll never be out in time tomorrow.'

The flap of the tent next to Seth's opened and a voice hissed, 'Will you two shut up? Some of us are trying to sleep!'

'You shouldn't have your head at the flap end, Tashelle, then you wouldn't have heard anything,' Seth called back in a loud whisper.

Tashelle grunted and zipped the flap back up.

They kissed once more before parting and making their way to their tents. Seth waited until Daisy was safely in her tent before entering his.

He hadn't even zipped his tent up when he heard the exclamation of despair and ran across to Daisy's tent as she backed out. 'What's up?'

'My sleeping bag is soaking, like someone threw a bucket of water over it!'

Seth went in with his torch, feeling around. Sure enough, it was sopping wet, as was the bottom of the tent. He shuffled out backwards.

'Nothing for it. There's a spare sleeping bag in the trailer. You can share with me.'

Daisy arched her eyebrows. 'You're forward.'

'Don't worry, it's purely a convenient

arrangement. I promise.' He drew a diagonal cross on his chest with his forefinger.

'I'm kidding. Thanks. It'll be a bit cosy though.'

'All the better,' he laughed.

7

Daisy opened one eye carefully, her eyelids stuck together as if with glue. Finally, getting both eyes open, she lifted her arm from inside the sleeping bag. Ten past seven. Urgh. Nearly time to rise, if not shine.

Seth, on her left, was facing away from her, his back right up close to her hip. She could hear his gentle breathing and almost fancied she could feel his warmth through the two sleeping bags, though it was highly improbable. The air, however, was warmer than it had been yesterday morning in her tent. Cosy and snug, that's how she felt.

She twisted as best she could to lie on her back, putting her hands behind her head and looking up into the darkness. It was weird not waking to a stocking. Her mum still put one together for her — sophisticated chocolates and toiletries these days — even though Daisy had pointed out she was a grown-up now. She knew Mum loved picking little gifts and wrapping them in tissue paper. She'd sent one down to London for her but Daisy hadn't wanted to bring it here. She'd save it for New Year.

At home, after going through the stocking, she would get dressed in a pretty frock, then go down for the Christmas morning sparkling wine cocktail. That was Dad's department. They would sit in the living room with the drink and home-made pastries, while they unwrapped their presents.

A twinge of nostalgia and longing rippled through her. It wasn't as if she was missing it completely, though. They were going to repeat it on New Year's Day for her.

From outside the tent there came a rustling and then a clank. Daisy sat bolt upright, listening. Was someone wetting more sleeping bags? Stealing the finds? She knelt forward, using the small torch Callie had loaned her. When she found

117

the zip she undid it as quietly as she could. With only a little bit opened, she peered out to see a torchlight swinging. A figure moved to the centre of the camp, knelt down and poked at a fire.

Rich. Of course. What was wrong with her? He was apparently always up first on the digs. And it wasn't as if there was anyone on the island to be creeping around secretly. Apart from Angus. Her sleep-addled brain had already made up a story worthy of the thriller section.

'What's up?' came a whisper.

Daisy twisted round, unable to make Seth out, but presuming he was lying down still by the sound of his voice.

'I heard something outside, but it's just Rich,' she murmured back.

'Why not come and give me a hug? We've still got ten minutes or so.'

She did as he asked, lying into his outstretched arm and cuddling into his chest.

'Happy Christmas.'

'And Happy Christmas to you too.' She kissed his chin, the highest she could reach. 'What would you be doing if your parents were at home and you were too?'

'Let's see. They'd go off to the church service and I'd go for a walk in the nearby woods. Karen, my sister, would have been up since six watching all the children's Christmas programmes, even though she's in her twenties — and working through the chocolate in her stocking. But the last time that happened was three years back, before Karen got married.'

Daisy giggled. 'You still have stockings too?'

'Courtesy of Grannie and Grandpa Simsek. There'll be one waiting for me now even though I won't get it until New Year. They're staying with Aunty Jean this year.'

She snuggled in a little further, feeling less childish, and more part of a lovely tradition.

'Dad would have prepared everything before church,' Seth carried on, 'so it was all either cooking or ready to be cooked.'

'Your dad?'

Seth tutted. 'So much surprise at men cooking. Honestly, which planet have you grown up on?'

'One where men don't cook!' She imagined Matt's reaction to Seth's statement. 'It's not a criticism. I think it's great.'

They lay silent for a while. The last of her stresses about missing the family Christmas or the one with Callie and the others drained away. She'd enjoyed the last two days, the tense expectation of a find, the excitement as an item emerged. It was thrilling just thinking about it. She'd miss it when she left here and went back to uni, simply to sit in a lecture room to learn.

Would she ever get this opportunity again?

Well, why not? A sketchy idea began to form.

'Right, let's get this show on the road,' said Seth, kissing the top of her head one more time before lifting them both to a sitting position.

'If we must.'

'You get dressed first.' He shuffled over to the tent flap, unzipped it and stretched, before crawling out in his joggers and T-shirt.

Letting herself out of the tent five minutes later, she found she had an audience. Each had a slightly different expression, though most could be summed up as surprised. Only Tashelle's face displayed a look that suggested she'd like to throw something at her.

Daisy attempted to lighten the mood with, 'Happy Christmas, everyone,' only to be interrupted by Tashelle.

'It didn't take you long to get your feet under the table. Or inside the sleeping bag.'

Daisy looked round for Seth. He'd maybe gone for a wash in the tiny stream, leading down from Stow Rise, as he had yesterday. Brrr! She'd waited for the kettle to boil and had taken the bowl behind her tent when it was her turn, and she'd do the same today.

'Someone . . . well, when I got into

my tent last night, my sleeping bag was soaking. No one else was up and I had to sleep somewhere, so I squashed in with Seth.'

'You started that with someone,' said Tashelle. 'Are you suggesting one of us was responsible?'

Henry stood up, knocking his cup clanging to the ground. 'This is serious. It didn't rain and these tents are stormproof even if it had.'

'Oh come on, Henry,' said Tashelle. 'She probably had a bottle of water in there the night before and didn't screw the lid on properly.'

Daisy knew it would be easier to ignore Tashelle's comment, but she was already defending herself before she'd thought it out.

'In that case I would have felt the wet yesterday morning. And I didn't have water in there anyway.'

Tashelle, about to open her mouth once again, was stilled by Henry's hand. 'That's enough, Tashelle. Daisy, come and sit down. Seth's sleeping arrangements are his business. I take my hat off to anyone willing to share one of these.' He pointed to the minuscule tents. 'It must have been a tight squeeze.'

Freja laughed. 'Shouldn't think there'd even be room for any hanky panky!'

'You'd be surprised,' Tashelle muttered.

'I'm sure I don't want to know your sordid night-time pastimes.'

'Whose sordid night-time pastimes?' Seth appeared, towel and washbag in one hand.

'Daisy was telling us about her damp tent.' Rich pointed to the rock. 'Better get the bag out and stick it over there. At least the heat here might dry it a little. There's no rain forecast today, but it might get a bit misty later.'

'So what did you sleep in, if your bag was wet?' Tashelle was not going to let this rest.

'The spare one in the trailer,' said Seth. 'Good job Rich thought to put it in.'

'Yes, Rich is a brilliant organiser.'

Henry tapped him on the shoulder, where he was hunkered down stirring the pot. 'I'm very thankful to have him on my team.'

Henry went back to his tent, so didn't hear Rich mutter, 'Not thankful enough to promote me.'

A slight shift in Seth's expression suggested he had heard. He said nothing, going to his tent.

Freya leaned over to Daisy.

'This is jolly, isn't it? Bad feeling flying all over the shop. And on Christmas Day, too.'

'Is it always like this on digs?'

'It varies. Depends on the personalities and current irritations. Well, I've got something to cheer things up . . . ' She reached into her bag and pulled out several bags of chocolate that included coins and reindeer. She placed them on the large, flat rock. 'Happy Christmas, everyone.'

Daisy smiled. 'That's very kind of you.'

Tashelle looked down on them and

pulled a face. 'Not for me. I don't put rubbish in my body.'

Freja ignored the remark. 'Ah, breakfast is ready. A nice bowl of porridge is what I need.'

Daisy followed Freja's lead, taking the offered porridge. It would set her up for whatever occurred on this cold, alien Christmas Day.

* * *

Christmas Day was not shaping up to be as Daisy had imagined. A few hours at close quarters with Seth had seemed compensation for family, the big seasonal meal and the fun and games. But here she was, stuck with Tashelle, who was clearly gloating about her separation from Seth.

'Them's the breaks, kid,' said Tashelle unable to stop herself from smirking as they set off through the greenery up the slight incline. 'If Henry wants Rich to give Seth a second opinion about the Bronze Age pots in Trench 1, there's not a lot you can do. No point brooding about it.'

Far from brooding, Daisy had been determined to present an upbeat response.

'I haven't complained, have I? I'm quite happy to help somewhere else, experience other trenches.'

'Trench 3 is the monks' burial ground, so there are bones. I hope you're not squeamish.'

'I'm a biology student, remember?' Eager to move away from Tashelle's barbed comments, she asked, 'So this is Stow Rise?' She looked up to the low peak of the hill.

'Yeah. 'Stow' means a holy place. Guess the monks thought it was.'

Being the nearest trench to the camp it took them little more than five minutes to reach it. Tashelle placed the boxes she'd been carrying on the edge of the trench and looked round.

'You can dig over there.' Tashelle pointed to a corner furthest from where items had already been found. 'That should keep you busy.'

Daisy had the distinct impression she was being shoved to where she was unlikely to find anything. So be it. She wasn't going to argue. If Tashelle was that bothered about gaining the glory for uncovering the next item, let her have it. Daisy took the trowel and brush given to her by Seth out of her waterproof pocket and crouched down in the naughty corner, as she thought of it.

It was brighter than yesterday, the white clouds more scattered, but it was colder. Daisy zipped her coat up though she'd have preferred to remove it to work. Hopefully it wouldn't be long before she warmed up with the exertion of digging.

'I hear you've only known Seth a few days,' Tashelle called over from her spot in the trench.

She could only have heard that from Freja, whether directly or otherwise.

'That's true, but he's good friends with my flatmates.' Really, she didn't see why she had to defend herself. She should just say, *What of it? Mind your own business*, but she'd been raised to be polite, only losing her temper if pushed. 'How many digs have you been on?' she said, hoping it would invite Tashelle to talk about herself, since it seemed to be her favourite subject.

'No time for chit-chat. We need to get on.'

It was on the tip of her tongue to say, *But you started it*. Nope. She wouldn't rise to it Tashelle was maybe hoping she would so she could have an argument.

Digging in silence suited Daisy, although it wasn't really silent at all, with the slight breeze rustling the grasses and the piping rasp of the oystercatchers somewhere overhead. Those sounds were relaxing, soothing Daisy's irritation. She began to wonder what the monks here did to mark Christmas Day, all those hundreds of years ago. If indeed they did anything.

Her trowel came up against something firm. She took a closer look. It was a creamy-grey colour, probably the rock here, though it was a little lighter. About to dig the trowel in to remove it, she stopped herself. What if it was something more significant? They'd found bones here, remarkably preserved in the favourable conditions of the soil, though no whole skeletons. She kept digging, deciding it was more likely some rock. She didn't want to give Tashelle any reason to mock her.

A little further down, she found the side of whatever it was. A long rock? Burrowing now in the other direction, she eventually came to another side of a slender item — part of a humerus bone, she was sure.

The excitement made her giddy. She'd found her very own monk, with a bone that looked remarkably preserved, even compared to the others. She'd better get Tashelle over, otherwise she'd never hear the last of it.

She lifted her head to find Tashelle knelt right over, concentrating on a small piece of ground.

'I think I've found something,' she called over.

Tashelle didn't even bother lifting her head. 'What now, a plant root or a stone?'

'Um, no. It looks like a bone.'

'And how would you know?' She looked up with a huff. 'OK, I guess I'd better humour you.'

She hauled herself up and stomped over, almost pushing Daisy out of the way to see what she'd found. Her expression suggested she was about to deliver a rebuke but then she froze for some seconds.

'Oh.' She scraped around it a little more. 'It's a humerus. That's an upper arm bone to you.'

'I know what it is.'

'Yeah. Right, I'll take over. Don't want some amateur clumsy-clogs chopping bits off. I haven't seen any bones as well preserved as this. Maybe the soil here . . .' She tailed off. 'I wonder. Perhaps if you start scraping here.' She pointed to an area only about a foot away, but further down, where the legs would have been if it was a whole skeleton. Unlikely. Everything else they'd found, even on the first dig, had been only small parts.

They weren't scraping for long when it became apparent that there was indeed a leg. Whether it belonged to the arm they'd yet to discover, but if it did, the body appeared to have been buried at an odd angle. She knew little about Saxon monks so it might have been their way of doing things.

They worked in silence as they concentrated on their task, Tashelle so engrossed she'd forgotten to scold Daisy every five minutes. Doggedly they kept going, Daisy not even checking the time until Seth appeared through the tall grasses.

'Hey, you two, it's lunchtime.'

Tashelle announced, 'There's a whole skeleton!' even though they'd only found part of one. Daisy had no doubt she was quick off the mark so it would seem like her discovery.

'Who found it first?' Seth lowered

himself into the trench to take a closer look.

Daisy looked at Tashelle who'd pulled her lips into a thin line, as was her habit when she didn't like something.

'Daisy found something white, but it was me who realised what it was.'

'To be fair, I did think it was a humerus, but didn't say because you're the expert.'

'So what have we got?' Seth hunkered down. He whistled out a long note. 'A skull, spine, one arm, one leg and part of another, by the looks of it.' He rubbed his chin, screwing his eyes up in concentration, before taking the phone from his pocket to use the torch. He bent down to take a better look. 'Mmm.' He stood up. 'Interesting.'

'What is?' said Daisy, though she had an inkling what he was getting at.

'Come and get lunch then I'll return with you after. We'd best get Freja to photograph it in situ.'

At the camp, nobody was interested in lunch once they heard of the find. Rushing together to the site, they chatted eagerly.

'It's not clear how old it is,' Seth told them when they arrived. 'We'd have to get it dated. It's in much better condition than the other bones.'

'Perhaps the soil's more peaty here,' Freja suggested as she started taking photos. Daisy noticed she pointed the camera at them too.

'Maybe.' Seth didn't sound at all sure. 'There's something different. I could be wrong, but . . .'

Here it comes, thought Daisy.

'You think so too, then?' said Tashelle.

'For crying out loud, just spit it out!' Freja bellowed at them.

Tashelle knelt down next to the remains. 'I should think you could see it for yourself, if you looked carefully. I bet even the biology undergraduate could spot it.'

Daisy bit her bottom lip before announcing, 'The pelvis and eye sockets suggest it's a woman. I would have thought that was unusual in a monastery. Unless there were nuns too.'

'I guess it's possible,' said Seth. 'There were monasteries that housed nuns as well as monks in the early days. And there are a number of gravestones for women at Lindisfarne, though we don't really know what their place was.'

'We can't be sure this person was even buried at the same time as the others,' Rich said, bending beside Tashelle to take a closer look. 'We can't be sure of anything until we get it dated properly. What do you think, Henry?'

Their leader was standing further back than the rest of them, one arm hugging his chest, the elbow of the other resting on it. 'Like you say, Rich, we'll have to wait and see. I don't think it's going anywhere. Let's eat lunch now so we have a couple of hours before the sun starts setting.'

His lack of enthusiasm surprised

Daisy as they dragged themselves back to camp.

'Something else I noticed . . . ' Daisy said tentatively, not wanting to tread on anyone's toes.

'Go on then, Miss Biology,' said Tashelle.

'The upper arm . . . I could be wrong . . . '

'A break that hadn't healed properly?' Seth offered.

Tashelle tutted. 'Well, of course I noticed that.'

'Lunch now, work later,' Henry insisted, hurrying ahead.

★   ★   ★

Daisy ended up working the rest of the day with Tashelle, but she didn't mind. Seth and Rich were uncovering their own big find in the Bronze Age trench, with lots of what looked like jewellery.

'So what do you hope to get out of this trip?' Tashelle asked as they worked on recovering more of the skeleton.

'I'm not sure I had anything in mind, apart from doing something outside the box, as it were.'

'That's what I thought on my first dig. It was a school trip after exams, Nottingham Castle. It was nice weather though, sunny, long days to work and socialise. Not sure how I'd have felt if I'd ended up in the back of beyond in December. It's not even dig season, but here we are.'

Daisy wondered why Tashelle had come if she felt like that. To see Seth? She might have her all wrong and it could simply be loyalty to Henry. You couldn't tell with her.

'It's good that you turned up to support Henry.'

'Yeah, well, he's a funny old stick, but he's a good professor and has always given us all lots of support during our time at uni,' she replied.

It was refreshing to see a different side of Tashelle, while it lasted. Daisy put down the trowel and brush for a moment to remove her coat.

'It's amazing how warm you get, doing this.'

'It sure is,' said Tashelle, removing her own coat. 'Won't be long before we can lift these items and box them up — and hide them in case Sir James comes back early.'

'Is he likely to do that?'

'I've no idea. Hopefully Angus would be able to warn us if that happened. I like him, but he's quite a character, isn't he?'

'I think I'd be too if I'd been brought up here, only my parents and tutor for company, no friends to play with. No wonder he lives in Newcastle now . . . Oh, hold on a sec . . . What's this?'

Tashelle stopped brushing at the soil to lean over. Daisy worked at the object for a while before losing confidence. It was metal, possibly delicate.

'Perhaps you'd better take over, Tashelle.'

The other woman nodded, taking Daisy's place.

Bit by bit she revealed a ring of

137

metal, not as delicate as Daisy had feared, but dirt-encrusted. As Tashelle brushed the metal it became clear the item was jewellery — and gold at that.

'It's a bracelet,' Tashelle said, turning the band round. 'And a late Bronze Age one at that.'

'So the skeleton is Bronze Age, not seventh century, like the monks?'

Tashelle looked down at the Lady of Sealfarne, as they'd nicknamed her at lunchtime.

'I wouldn't like to say. Let's get this out and packed up as quickly as we can. It'll be sundown soon and I don't want to be stuck here in the dark.' She shivered.

Daisy shivered too, though she'd no idea why. Camp was only five minutes away, and they had a torch, but she felt the same uneasiness.

★   ★   ★

The sun had disappeared below the low hump of Stow Rise as Tashelle and

Daisy carefully placed the last of the artefacts into the box.

'The others will be amazed by the bracelet,' Tashelle said. 'What on earth is it doing here?'

'You mean, what *in* earth.' Daisy laughed, cheered no end by the find.

'If you can't take it seriously, you shouldn't be here,' Tashelle snapped.

'I do take it seriously, Tashelle. It's fascinating. A conundrum. If it's Bronze Age, the Lady of Sealfarne's, was this already a burial ground when the monks arrived? And did they know that? Could she even be Iron Age, or a Saxon, with a Bronze Age bracelet?'

'A little knowledge is a dangerous thing,' Tashelle quoted, clearly irritated. 'I'll take this box, you take that one.'

'Just thinking out loud.'

'You leave the thinking to the experts and let's get going. Shoot, I can barely see this path in the twilight. You lead the way.'

So if there's anything in the way, I'll trip up first. 'OK,' Daisy said as cheerily

139

as she could, not wanting Tashelle to know she was getting to her.

Arriving at the camp without incident, they found they were the only ones there, though the fire was burning and with a pot hanging over it.

'We'll put the boxes over there.' Tashelle pointed to one of two large rocks. 'Then I've got to see to a call of nature.' She hurried off though the vegetation to the powder room.

Daisy walked over to Seth's tent, remembering her trainers were still in there from this morning. Having retrieved them, she sat in the doorway of his tent to take off her walking boots and put the trainers on. She'd barely slipped the second one on when she found herself suddenly in a heap among the sleeping bags and smothered by the tent. There was a weight on her, holding her down, but she managed a muffled screech before the weight lifted and she screamed in earnest. She heaved herself into a sitting position, hair sticking out of the scrunchy she'd tied it up with, catching her breath.

She heard two voices, one of them Seth shouting, 'What's wrong?' and Tashelle's yelling, 'What the blazes is it now?'

Seth reached her first, helping her out of the tent. Tashelle was quickly by his side.

'What happened?' he asked.

'I — I don't know. I came in here to get my trainers and was putting them on when something jumped on me.'

Tashelle chuckled. 'What, like Big Foot?'

Seth frowned at her. 'This is no time to take the mickey.'

'Someone then, I don't know.' Daisy brushed imaginary dust from her jeans.

Seth looked at Tashelle. 'Where were you?'

'What? You think it was me? We walked back together. I only went to the powder room.'

'You're the only other one here.'

'As are you,' Tashelle pointed out. 'And where's Rich? Wasn't he working with you?'

'He left earlier, to collect any rabbits that had been trapped. You can see, he's

141

been preparing it.' He pointed to the fire.

Seth and Tashelle glared at each other, in a stand-off neither seemed inclined to lose. It wasn't until Freja came running through the vegetation from the path to Trench 2, her camera bag flapping, that they looked away.

'What was that screaming?'

'Daisy was attacked in my tent,' Seth told her.

'What? Who by?'

'You're alone?' Tashelle said accusingly.

'You're not suggesting I had something to do with it, are you?' Freja put her camera bag down. 'I've only just arrived back from Trench 2.'

Seth picked up a box. 'Let's get these artefacts and this equipment in one place, shall we? So where's Henry? Not that I'm accusing him of anything,' he added quickly.

'Covering the trench over with a tarpaulin. He reckons it's going to rain tonight and he's only half-uncovered something. I went off to take photos of the sunset.'

Daisy looked west, at the pinky orange of the clear sky. 'Rain. Really?'

'He's invariably right,' said Tashelle. 'That'll be fun. Still, at least your tent should be dry now, so you won't have to share.'

More's the pity, thought Daisy. And there had to be safety in numbers.

It wasn't long before Henry and Rich turned up, coming from different directions. Daisy told her story once more. Rich held up a sack bag and explained he'd been at the cliffs searching for scurvy grass to put in the stew. 'For Vitamin C.'

Henry shook his head. 'I don't like the sound of this. I'm wondering whether we should take what we've found and cut our losses.'

Everyone except Daisy raised an objection.

'No way,' Tashelle said. 'Not after what Daisy and I found today.'

Equal billing from Tashelle? It was like a bizarre Christmas present! Things were looking up. Tashelle went to one of their boxes and brought back the gold bracelet. 'This was near to our Lady of Sealfarne. She must have been important.'

There were exclamations of wonder and delight as they all gathered round.

Only the professor remained where he was.

'What's wrong, Prof?' Rich asked Henry.

'I'm wondering if someone knows about this bracelet, or suspects it's here, and wants to steal it for themselves.'

Freja turned to face Henry. 'Do you think that's why Angus was so keen to get us here? After all, he might remember there being a bracelet, and maybe other jewellery among the finds.'

'Except we didn't find any jewellery in the original dig,' Henry said.

'You didn't find a near complete skeleton either, but it was there.'

'Hang on, hang on,' Seth said. 'Think about it . . . If Angus knew about it and wanted it for himself, why would he risk bringing us here? Surely he'd hire a digger and get it over here himself, like his father did thirty years back.'

'Is it possible — ' Daisy started, disconcerted to find all eyes on her. 'That is, could it be that someone in the original team found the bracelet, and possibly other items, and kept them hidden?'

'Then how would it have ended up back in the ground, brain box?' Tashelle tutted.

Business as usual, then. The new Tashelle didn't last long.

'Don't be so rude, Tashelle,' Freja said. 'She's putting ideas out there, like the rest of us. We'd better keep these finds close by, take them with us tomorrow if necessary.'

Tashelle groaned. 'What a drag.'

'There's nothing we can do about it for now,' Henry decided. 'So let's have a look at what else was found today, while Rich finishes up.'

When the men moved away to fetch the boxes, Tashelle muttered, 'I don't like the way this is turning out.'

Freja rubbed her hands together. 'Ooh, I do. All my Christmases have come at once.'

'Yeah, that's what worries me.'

★ ★ ★

Darn Freja and her obsession with photographing every last clod of earth. OK, maybe he was exaggerating, thought Rich as he dug the point of his trowel into the soggy earth the following day, but he really could do with a little help right now, digging in the monastery ruins.

Henry had swapped trenches with him for the day, clearly lured by the finds at Trench 3. Rich had already missed out on finding the Lady of Sealfarne yesterday after being swapped with Daisy, but he was pretty pleased with himself now after what he'd just dug up. It was one in the eye for Henry, who'd be miffed he hadn't been the one to find the silver cup. It was the first silver item they'd found. There might be others, part of an altar set, and he

146

was eager to find out.

The monastery area was close to the southern point with its cliffs, and there was a north-eastern wind blowing across it, preventing him removing his coat, which made digging cumbersome.

Henry had been right. It had rained last night, a downpour beating on their tents, so he'd slept little after that, and it was taking its toll now.

He slipped his mobile out of his back pocket. Four minutes past ten . . . was that all? He yawned, stood up and stretched his back, looking forward to showing off the cup to the others — and Daisy. Nice girl. Shame there weren't more like her in his department. Seth was lucky if he'd hooked up with her. He and Tashelle had never been a fit in his opinion.

'Right, back to work,' he ordered himself.

There was a stubborn piece of pottery he wanted to get out now. No more metal at the moment, more's the pity, but there might be some beneath this. It had been a weird find, that bracelet in this trench with the Lady of Sealfarne, though he couldn't put his finger on why.

'Ah, there you are, my beauty.' Rich pulled out the reluctant pottery, a fragment of a pot he reckoned, with a rim of some sort. He lifted it to the light, turning it to examine it.

There was a sound, like a twig snapping. Odd. There weren't any trees or bushes here, though he guessed some of the gorse might snap if you broke a stem off. Maybe Freja had finally returned. Rich looked round. In the distance, dark shapes were moving among the waves. Seals.

He climbed out of the trench, heading to the clear plastic box they were storing the items in, and laid the pottery down carefully. After pressing the lid back on, he picked up the water bottle next to it. He wove through gorse and wind-dried grasses to the edge of the cliffs to take a better look at the seals while he quenched his thirst.

A combination of grey and white clouds moved rapidly across the sky, covering and revealing the sun every few seconds. Overhead, a few oyster-catchers glided on the wind. To his right he spotted the mouth of the Stowborn stream, cascading down into the sea. It would be a lovely spot in the summer.

Stepping forward he peered over the cliffs to see if he could spot the eider ducks Henry had mentioned resided here.

Was that . . . ?

'Whoooooooa!'

Rich's feet slithered on the wet rock and moss. He had just about managed to save himself when his other leg buckled beneath him and he slipped.

'Oh — my — ahhh!'

He stumbled down the cliff, attempting to grab at a protruding rock before he fell completely.

8

Freja considered the empty trench. Rich had clearly had made quite a find, with the silver cup taking pride of place in the box. Fancy just leaving it here and walking off. It was tempting to pinch it, just to teach him a lesson!

She picked it up and turned it round to examine it. Nice piece. She could just picture his face when he found it gone. It would make great TV. She lifted her camera, taking photos of it, then filmed round the trench. She kept the camera rolling as she walked towards the cliffs, filming the rapidly moving clouds. Panning around she stopped for a while when the small waterfall came into sight, bringing the camera back to the cliffs once more.

The voice sounded like a gull initially, until she realised it was Rich's voice calling.

'Help! I'm here, over here! Over the cliff!'

She couldn't help laughing at the comedy of it all — until she skirted the gorse to get to the edge. Rich was hanging on with one hand, trying to find something to grab hold of with the other. She emitted a strong Swedish expression before saying, 'What the hell are you doing, Rich?'

'Oh, ya know, just hanging around, having the craic. I fell, obviously. I'm hanging on by a thread here and my hand's going numb, so do you think, if you're not too busy, you could help me up?'

This was simply too good an opportunity to miss. Freja pointed the camera at him.

'For pity's sake, Freja, put that thing away! I'm going to fall soon if you don't help me.'

Freja lowered the camera. 'It's only about five metres down. Don't make such a fuss.'

'Only five . . . ? It's sheer and there

are rocks at the bottom. Now get me out of here!'

Fun over, she supposed. She put the camera to one side, taking hold of his arms.

'Push against the cliff with your feet and walk up as I pull you.'

'I'll try.'

He did as she asked and she managed to get him up pretty easily. When he was two-thirds the way over the cliff, he collapsed on the rock. She pulled him up by his jeans the rest of the way.

'It's a good job I do weights at the gym,' she said, laughing.

He rested on the rock on his front, breathing heavily. Freja sat with her ankles crossed, knees pointing up, staring at him.

'You all right? You have to be careful here.'

He rolled onto his back. 'I thought I was being careful. In fact, I know I was.'

'What are you saying, Rich?'

'Did you ever do that trick when you

were a child, where you karate chop be-hind someone's knees and they collapse?'

She scrunched up her forehead, looking at him as if he was speaking gibberish.

'No. That must be an English thing.'

'I'm Irish.'

'That too. I'm here now, so no one's going to creep up on you and karate chop anything.'

He gave a look that seemed to say, *Unless it was you who did it*. She waited for the accusation but it never materia-lised.

He propped himself up. 'I've been waiting ages for you to get back. Come and see what I found.'

She didn't admit she'd already seen it.

★ ★ ★

'All I'm saying Rich, is that, by your own admission, you were half asleep.' Tashelle was not showing any sympathy for Rich's incident as she handed him a sandwich. 'You probably just slipped,

153

like Freja said, and didn't realise.'

'I was not half asleep, I was just a bit tired.'

'That's a heck of a bruise on your cheek,' Seth said, in an effort to break up the bad feeling. 'I've some arnica cream in my bag you can put on it.'

'I'll be all right. I've smothered the scrapes in antiseptic — now that did hurt.'

'I bet.' Seth looked up at Freja as she joined the group round the dead fire. 'Did you see anyone else on your travels? I mean . . . '

'You mean any of us not where we should have been?' Freja replied.

'Not necessarily. There's Angus too.'

'Tashelle was on a comfort break twice when I visited Trench 3.'

'I told you, Freja, I seem to have a problem today, so don't keep on,' Tashelle growled. 'Probably something in the water.'

'That we brought over from the mainland and we're all drinking,' Freja retorted.

Henry butted in with, 'I can confirm that Tashelle wasn't long each time she went.'

'But she didn't appear at all when I came to take photos the second time,' Freja said. 'That could have been the time that Rich was attacked.'

'It was too early, from what Rich said.'

'But Freja, you said before that you reckoned he'd simply slipped.' Tashelle's voice rose.

'I'm not making any judgments, just throwing ideas out there.'

'Henry went for comfort breaks too, but you're not suggesting he went to push people off cliffs.'

'Perish the thought!' Freja laughed.

'It's not funny. And what about you two?' Tashelle pointed at Seth and Daisy, sitting together silently.

'I don't think either of us went anywhere.' Seth glanced at Daisy who shook her head.

'What, in the whole four hours?' Tashelle said.

'That's right,' Daisy said. 'I was bursting for the loo when I got back here, though.'

Tashelle pulled her tall frame up to its full height. 'You see, now this is the problem. What if people are working together? Daisy says she's only just met Seth and has no reason to hamper the dig, but what if Seth has her here as an accomplice?'

As several voices piped up to dis-agree, Henry stood, clapping his hands to silence them.

'I've heard enough. If this carries on I will insist on us leaving the island. We can't work together if we don't even trust each other.'

Everyone looked round at each other.

'I mean it. If I hear about one more incident, I'm packing up and leaving.'

Freja, next to Henry, took his arm. 'But you've waited so long to return. It would be a shame.'

'I should have left this particular bit of the past in the past. I won't sacrifice the good working relationship of any of my team. And if there's someone else on the island, or Angus is messing around, we'd be better off out of it.'

Good working relationship. Seth considered the words. He and Tashelle hadn't worked particularly well together the last year. When Freja belonged to the department, she'd got on a lot of people's nerves — more so now with her ridiculous TV programmes. Rich had been off with him and Henry since Seth had got the promotion. Despite all this, they'd managed to keep a lid on it, for the most part, even on the dig last summer in Italy.

'It's a shame the trenches aren't closer,' Tashelle said. 'We could look out for each other.'

Freja huffed out a brief laugh. 'Keep an eye on each other, you mean.'

'I'm warning you.' Henry picked up his bag of tools. 'Now, I don't know about you lot, but I want to get another couple of hours in before it starts to get dark. And it'll be earlier today with this cloud cover. Freja, I want you to work

157

with me this afternoon on Trench 2. Rich, you go back to Trench 3 with Tashelle,' he said before he strode off, leaving half his sandwich uneaten.

Freja regarded the group, lifting her eyes to the sky in irritation. 'Is he trying to keep an eye on me?' She ran off after Henry, muttering in disgruntled Swedish.

Rich watched them from his seat, his mouth bunched up and his arms crossed.

'Yeah, that's right, Henry, now I've found a nice silver cup at Trench 2, you go and find the rest,' he muttered. 'Chasing the glory.'

When they'd disappeared from sight, Rich leant down with difficulty and picked up a folder behind his chair. 'What's this?' He opened it, flicking through, then seemed to be taken by one particular piece of paper.

'Trench records I imagine,' Tashelle concluded.

'Something like that.'

'Henry's right about getting on, though.' Seth picked up his sandwich.

'Are you going to rest up for a while, Rich?'

It was a few seconds before Rich replied to Seth, concentrating as he was on the papers.

'Mm? What? No, I'm most certainly not. I'm sore but I'm not kicking my heels around here all day.' He put the papers away and stood as if his bones were stiff. 'This is Henry's. I'll shove it back in his tent.'

As Seth walked away from camp with Daisy, he saw Rich hesitate by Henry's tent and get his phone out. What was that all about? Tashelle was nearby, collecting people's rubbish from lunch, moaning about the mess.

Boy, would he be glad when this dig was over!

★ ★ ★

Tashelle peered over at Rich who was swearing mildly as he opened up his bag of tools at the monks' burial ground.

159

'What's up now?' she said, straightening herself from where she'd just knelt down.

'Seth's gear. How the hell did it get in here?' He held up a rolled-up piece of hessian that was filled with tools.

Tashelle would have recognised it even if Rich hadn't named the owner. Seth was particular about his tools. His mother had apparently run this up on her sewing machine in Seth's second year of uni. It reminded her of the knitting needle roll her nan used to have.

'And he'll realise they're missing out of his back pack just about now.' She jumped up. 'I'll take them over to him in Trench 1. I could do with a run. I haven't had one since we arrived here.'

'With good reason. You can't run on this rocky terrain, with all this out-of-control vegetation. You've walked the tracks, you know what they're like. You'll end up looking like me.' He pointed to his burgeoning bruises.

'Give it here.' She plucked the tool roll from his hands. 'It'll only take me a few minutes there and back.' She did up her jacket. 'This breeze is chilling. The run will hopefully warm me up too. See ya in ten, tops.'

'Yeah, and the rest,' he called after her.

The first few seconds of running weren't too bad, but she soon realised Rich was right. Just walking some of these paths was hard enough. The track here was merely a gap they'd pushed through to get to the site. She slowed down but was determined to keep up a trot.

She came to the camp, running past it and onto the path leading to Trench 1. Even on this, nothing more than a trampled trail through the vegetation made by the Jeep, bits of rock and stone made it hard to run. It wasn't long before her foot twisted to one side and she had to stop.

'Ow! That's all I need.'

Her ankle was a little sore, but not too bad. She started off again, slower now. The gorse bushes were higher and she didn't want to fall into them, but neither did she want to be too long and have Rich say he told her so.

The path twisted slightly in the wrong direction here, before meeting the crossroads and heading back towards Trench 1. If she could go cross country a little, she'd be quicker. She headed in between the gorse bushes, careful not to get too close. The land headed uphill slightly here and she struggled up the loose stones. She stopped briefly, bending over to place her hands on her knees, closing her eyes, Seth's package still under her arm. The wind was whipping up now, blowing her hair all around her head. About to stand up, she found herself plunging forward, unable to stop herself.

'No!'

She closed her eyes, pulling up her arms to protect her face from the middle of several gorse bushes. Fighting against them to begin with, she soon realised it was the worst thing she could do. She lay still before opening her eyes tentatively to look for gaps where she could put her hands down safely. Pulling herself up slowly, she screamed as she was caught up in the prickly branches.

There were spines attached to several parts of her body and through her jeans. Covering her face had saved it from damage. She was crying by the time she'd disentangled herself from the bushes, limping back to the path and cursing her stupidity.

She'd better head back to camp nearby. If she could get a signal on the way she could phone one of the others, tell them what happened. If not, she'd make her way back to Rich.

Finally making it to the edge of camp, she was relieved to see Freja there, walking up and down with her mobile, lifting it to get a signal. She turned when she heard someone approaching.

'What on earth happened to you?' she said, eyes wide with horror. She came over, taking Tashelle's arm and leading her to the flat rock.

'I fell into the gorse bushes. I was going over to Trench 1, to take Seth's tools. Rich found them in his bag. But, I think, I think — '

Tashelle started crying, much to her own shame. She never cried in front of people.

'I think I might have been pushed. I don't know. It happened so fast. And the gorse bushes are easy to hide in.'

'Not another one!' Freja sighed. 'Sit down. I'll get the first aid box.'

Tashelle lowered herself cautiously until she felt the rock beneath her.

Freja fetched the first aid kit from the trailer.

'First of all, we need to get these thorns out of your arms.'

Tashelle's tears started again. What the hell would she look like in short sleeves?

'Don't you get your camera out to film this.'

There was a pause before Freja said, 'I had no intention of doing that.'

Freja used tweezers to remove several thorns, then dabbed Tashelle's arms and hands with the antiseptic. Next she started on her legs. It hurt, and she was cold from lifting her sweatshirt off and then pulling her jeans down. The tears disappeared and she felt the anger building. By the time Freja had finished, Tashelle's fury had fuelled her determination.

She jumped up from the rock, declaring, 'I'm going to Trench 1. That's where I was heading when this happened.'

'I'd stay here and rest if I were you. I'll go and tell Rich what's happened.'

'No! He's not sitting round like a victim, and I'm not going to either. Someone's playing silly beggars. Rich, me, Daisy . . . Though one of those might be a red herring to mislead us all.'

'Tash, you're not thinking straight.'

'On the contrary, it's as clear as day what's happening here.'

'Well, it's as clear as mud to me.'

Tashelle started to rush off, having to slow right down when she realised everything still hurt. She'd put up with that.

Freja followed. 'I'm not letting you go off on your own, Tash.'

Hobbling along the path, cursing under

her breath, she kept going. Freja by her side was trying to talk reason into her, but she was wasting her breath.

★ ★ ★

Daisy was concentrating hard on digging around the item Seth had been working on before lunch. He'd taken longer than she'd expected to find that his tools were missing from his backpack.

'Are you here alone?' Tashelle said.

Daisy looked up, surprised at a woman's voice, not Seth's. 'Hello, yes, Seth has — oh gosh, what's happened to you?'

Tashelle's hands were covered in scratches blood and there were blood stains on her jeans.

Freja explained about Tashelle falling in the gorse bushes while taking Seth's tools to him, but was interrupted by Tashelle herself.

'I didn't fall, I'm sure I didn't. How long have you been on your own?' Tashelle demanded.

'Um, fifteen, twenty minutes? Seth's tools weren't in his bag, so he assumed he'd left them at camp. Perhaps he didn't find them there.'

'We've just come from there and we didn't see him,' Tashelle said. 'Something mighty weird is going on here.'

'I agree,' Daisy said, joining them on the edge of the trench.

'I'm going back to the camp,' Tashelle yelled, limping off quickly, but soon slowing down.

'You should have stayed there to begin with,' Freja called, quickly catching her up.

Daisy, not wild about the idea of being at the trench on her own, followed them.

As they arrived at the camp, Seth was just coming out of his tent, scratching his head.

'There you are,' bawled Tashelle, limping ahead of them now.

'What on earth — '

'Happened to me?' She followed with a rambled version of her fight with the gorse bushes.

167

Seth shook his head. 'This isn't going to go down well with Henry. Are you sure you didn't trip? You shouldn't have been running on this terrain.'

'I know that now! And no, I don't think I tripped. Unless you also think Rich and your precious Daisy also tripped.'

Daisy tramped forward. 'I know what you're doing, you've been putting me down ever since I turned up.'

Tashelle ignored the comment, turning to Seth and stabbing a forefinger at his arm.

'And where have you been? Daisy said you came to camp to look for your tools, and you weren't here when we got here, nor on your way when we went to Trench 1.'

'I went to the beach on the way, to collect some supper. Look in the bucket if you don't believe me.'

The three women gathered round the yellow bucket, complete with water and shellfish.

'Hang on,' said Daisy. 'If you were coming over to with Seth's tools, then

168

where are they?'

'Oh, shoot!' Tashelle clenched her fist and thumped it against her thigh. 'Ouch! I shouldn't have done that.' She took a few seconds to recover. 'I must have dropped them in the bush when I fell over. I expect they'll still be there.'

'You'd better show us where,' said Seth. 'Otherwise I'll never get any work done.'

'Thanks for the sympathy.'

'Afterwards, I suggest you come back to the camp to rest,' Seth said.

'I'm fine. I can't leave Rich on his own.'

'And I'd better get back to Henry,' Freja said.

Tashelle took hold of Freja's arm. 'Can you leave off telling him what happened until supper time? I'll explain. I don't want him going off on one and insisting we all up sticks and leave.'

Freja didn't reply straight away. Eventually she said, 'Yah, OK.'

Tashelle managed to retrace her route just off the path and located the bushes she fell in, by the fact they were flattened on one side.

Seth knelt down to explore the ground. 'There they are. Luckily the roll's still done up so hopefully none have fallen out.' He lay on his stomach, wriggling beneath the uncrushed side and leaning in to retrieve his tools. 'Got them.'

'I'll get going,' said Tashelle, walking away.

She stopped suddenly.

They'd all heard it, the rustling. Daisy felt her body tense. Whoever it was, surely they wouldn't try anything with three of them there.

Seth put his finger to his lips to indicate quiet. They each turned their heads only to look around.

From out of the vegetation, and shooting across the path to cover again, came a fox.

Daisy let out the breath she hadn't realised she'd been holding in.

'I wonder if that's the one that makes all the noise?' Tashelle said. 'How the blazes did foxes even get on the island?'

Seth placed his tools in his backpack. 'Probably the same way as the rabbits

— hiding on a boat.'

'Could they have knocked into you and Rich?' Daisy suggested, not even convinced herself that it was a plausible explanation.

'And attacked you through the tent as well?' Seth raised his eyebrows.

'It's all right,' Tashelle said. 'She's just thinking aloud. She does that a lot.'

Seth looked confused. As Tashelle walked away, Daisy explained the conversation she'd had with Tashelle when working with her.

'Ignore her,' Seth said.

Easier said than done, thought Daisy.

★ ★ ★

Seth wasn't happy with what he was about to do. He surveyed his colleagues around the fire. Henry was only thinking of the welfare of the group he was in charge of, but . . .

But what? Someone was trying to scare them. Henry had spent more time than usual looking at his mobile, a piece

171

of technology that on the whole he objected to as distracting. None of them had managed to find a signal since they'd arrived, so if he was looking at any kind of messages they must be ones he'd received before getting here. Had someone been harassing him not to come to the island? Who, apart from Sir James MacKinnon and Lady MacKinnon, would object to them being here?

Lady MacKinnon. Neither Angus nor Henry had mentioned how she might feel about the dig, given that she'd been in favour of it all those years back. He had to speak up.

'Henry, I understand your concerns, but we've come too far to be frightened off. The fact that anyone wants to frighten us off — if they do — means there's something to hide and we need to see this through. If there isn't anyone, then these are all just accidents so we don't need to worry. I think we should take a vote.'

Henry bunched his lips up, staring into the fire. 'Do you all think we should vote on it?'

There were several murmurs of 'Yes.'

Daisy was the only one who didn't reply, no doubt thinking she had no say in it.

'If that's how you feel, then we'll take a vote.'

Seth shifted in his seat. 'OK. All those in favour of staying.' He put his hand up, as did Tashelle, Rich and Freja. 'All those in favour of leaving.'

Only Henry's hand went up. He looked at each of his department in turn with an expression that suggested they'd all betrayed him.

'So be it.'

He stood and walked towards his tent, stepping in and zipping it up.

Seth lowered his head and shook it.

'It's not your fault,' Daisy whispered, clutching his arm. 'Two of the people who were targeted have decided to stay.'

Seth lifted his arm to put it round her. 'What would you have voted for?'

'I would have voted to stay.'

'Even after the incident in the tent?'

'Especially after the incident in the tent. I don't want them getting away with it.'

'That's my reasoning. We should stay because someone's trying to get rid of us.'

Tashelle called over, 'What are you two whispering about? Planning your next move?'

'That's not helpful, Tashelle,' Rich said. 'Cup of tea, anyone?'

'Me, please.' Freja was the only one to reply. 'Only four more days. We're half way through.'

'Mercifully,' Tashelle said.

Rich poured water from the kettle into two cups. 'You didn't have to vote to stay.'

'I wanna know who did this to me, and why.'

'Ditto,' said Rich.

'I'm always up for solving a mystery,' Freja said. 'Let's hope our curiosity isn't our downfall.'

It was the thought Seth hadn't

wanted to voice, but now it was out there. He hoped they hadn't taken on more than they'd bargained for.

9

She wasn't sure how Seth was feeling about it, but Freja standing there filming them as they dug, was starting to get on Daisy's nerves. She didn't relish ending up on one of Freja's programmes. Not that anything interesting enough to televise was happening at that moment.

Henry had swapped them all around again today. After several significant finds in the Bronze Age trench by her and Seth yesterday, Henry had decided he wanted to work there, taking Freja with him. Rich had been right about him chasing the glory. Seth and Daisy were now at Trench 3, the monks' burial area, while Rich and Tashelle were at the Trench 2, the monastery ruins.

Seth was completely focussed on what he was doing, alternately sticking his trowel in the mud, scraping it and brushing it away. He may not even have realised

Freja was still there. She noticed he got like that when something in particular was grabbing his interest.

'Oh, wow!' Seth blurted out with some passion. 'This could be it!'

'Could be what?' Freja said, still filming.

Daisy left her digging to have a look.

'What is it?' She leant over, hands tucked between her knees. 'Another humerus?'

'Exactly. I reckon it could be the missing arm of our Lady of Sealfarne.'

'That would make it nearly complete,' she said.

Freja moved in closer, aiming her camera at the find. She put on quiet lilting tones. 'So this is possibly the missing arm of the skeleton we've named the Lady of Sealfarne,' she said, clearly for the camera.

Seth glanced at Daisy. 'I think at least the top half of the arm is here. Would you help me?'

Daisy fetched her tools and came back to start removing the earth further down, while Freja continued to walk round with the camera, alternating between photos and film footage.

'Darn it.' Freja removed the strap from around her neck and fiddled with the camera. 'The battery's run out, and I left the spare at camp. Don't go too fast, I'll run back and fetch it.'

'No, don't run,' said Seth. 'Look what happened to Tashelle. Whether she was pushed or not, she said she'd turned her ankle even before the incident. Just walk.'

'Yah, whatever. See you in a bit.'

When she was out of earshot, Seth said, 'Like we're going to go slower just to suit her. I can take the necessary shots on my phone as we're going along. I swear she thinks she'll get something from this for TV. Why else would she be here?'

'She told me she came as a favour to Henry.'

'I still think she's up to something.'

They worked on together, both thrilled as the bones of the lower arm were revealed. Daisy daydreamed about being the person to work on the skeleton once it was back in the lab. If only she'd had a better idea about archaeology when she'd applied to uni.

She was just making a start on where hopefully the hand would be when Freja came rushing back, out of breath.

'The camp, the camp — it's been ransacked!'

Seth stood bolt upright. 'What?'

'The pans, the wood, tents, sleeping bags . . . even my camera stuff — all over the place! Like someone was looking for something.'

Seth rubbed his forehead. 'The artefacts?'

'They're OK, but they were in the trailer. Maybe I disturbed whoever it was before they got them?'

'Why didn't you go straight to Henry?'

'Because . . . well, because I know you two were here when it happened. For all I know, it was one of the other three that did it.'

Seth looked like he was going to raise an argument against the idea, but he huffed out instead. 'I suppose it's not beyond the bounds of possibility,' he conceded. 'We'll come back with you, but we'd better take the boxes too.'

'I'll help,' Freja said, taking one of them.

She went on ahead, giving Daisy time to voice a thought she wasn't happy with.

'Is it possible that Freja did it herself?'

'Ransacked the place? What for? The finds are all at the trenches. Oh, unless she's creating a scenario to film.'

'That's what I was thinking.'

They had to go slowly through the plants, skirting gorse bushes with the boxes. At the camp they put them down and looked around the place.

'What a mess!' Seth said, picking up a sleeping bag and dusting it down before throwing it back into Henry's tent. 'Freja, would you go to Trench 1 and fetch Henry, please? Daisy and I will start clearing up.'

'Yah, of course.'

'I'd have gone myself,' he told Daisy after Freja left, 'but I didn't want to leave you here with her.'

'I don't think she'd do anything to me here, it'd be too obvious. And if it is her, she's only after causing a distraction, not up to anything sinister.'

'I'm not taking that risk.' He put his arms around her and gave her a quick kiss.

Henry was back within twenty minutes, hurrying the last few metres to the centre of camp, his face like thunder. 'I told you we should have left, but no, you all knew better.'

'Well we definitely can't leave now,' Freja said. 'There's something big going on here. I reckon it's got something to do with that skeleton Tash and Daisy found. Or that bracelet. Or both.'

Henry turned on her. 'This is not one of your silly TV shows, making up things to get people to watch. If I find out you're responsible for this . . .'

'Henry, how could you think that?'

'Shall we save our energy for clearing up?' Seth interrupted.

Henry walked away a few paces,

turning only to say, 'I'll trust this to you three. There's no point us all wasting our time on it. I was in the middle of digging something up. If we're going to stay here until the bitter end, let us at least have as much to show for it as possible. It should only take you until lunch time which is — ' He checked his watch. 'In fifty minutes.'

'You should have told him about the arm,' Freja said when he'd gone. 'That it might belong to the Lady of Sealfarne.'

Seth shook his head. 'Somehow I don't think it would have made any difference.'

* * *

The camp was cleared up by the time Tashelle and Rich returned, though there was enough out of place to show something had been going on.

'Have you been interfering with my stuff?' Tashelle barked at Daisy, the closest to her tent as she approached. Tashelle's tent zip was undone and some of her belongings, including a towel and makeup bag were in the opening.

'No, but someone ransacked the camp. We've mostly cleared up now.'

'For crying out loud!' Tashelle went into her tent, pulling in her belongings and tidying them.

'Was anything missing?' Rich asked.

'Nothing specific to the dig that we can tell,' Seth said, putting the pans near the fire. 'Individual property only each of you will know.'

'They even knocked the pans about!' Rich said, reorganising them as he liked them. 'Was it a search or an attempt to make us leave?'

'Who knows, Rich?'

Tashelle came out of her tent, saying, 'Who discovered it?'

'I did,' Freja said. 'When I came back for my spare camera battery.'

'How do we know you didn't do it, then?'

'You don't. But then, how do I know you didn't?'

'Because neither of us left our trench

long enough to get back here and do this,' Rich interrupted.

'You might have done it together.'

Seth walked between them.

'Enough! We need to stand together, and we definitely don't want Henry hearing us arguing.'

'Freja, are you in charge of lunch?' Rich asked.

'Sorry, I hadn't got round to doing it with all the mess.'

'I'm starving. I'll do it myself. It'll be quicker that way.' Rich bent to delve in the cool boxes they'd brought, buried into the earth. 'I've got soup in here, shop bought I'm afraid, but it'll do. I'll use the camping stove to make it quicker.'

Henry turned up a little late, ten minutes after, humping his boxes with him and putting them down next to the others. 'I could have done with you coming back to help me with these,' he told Freja, who was sitting round the stove.

'Sorry Henry, but you did tell me to help clear up here. It took a while.'

He didn't reply, sitting in the space next to Rich and taking the bowl of soup offered to him.

'Henry, did you notice anything amiss here from Trench 1?' Rich said.

'You can't see the camp from there.'

'True, but there might have been something untoward, or a noise . . . ?'

'I had my head down, concentrating on the job.' Henry shook his head as Rich offered him a spoon, then lifted the bowl to his lips.

'I think it might be a good idea,' Tashelle started, glancing at Seth, 'if Daisy stayed here to guard the camp. She's the only one who isn't an archaeologist, so we could be sure all the artefacts would be safe.'

Seth jumped in with, 'That's hardly fair.'

'No, it's fine,' Daisy said, though disappointed, especially now they'd found another piece of the skeleton. 'Tashelle's right. And I'm sure whoever did this to the camp won't be back, because they either found what they were looking for or they've realised it's not here. I'll get the fire going for this evening and make supper. There's rabbit left over from yesterday, yes?' She looked over to Rich.

'It's in a cool box, skinned and boned and ready to put in a stew. And there's plenty of veg, apart from the stuff you could go foraging for.'

Daisy felt almost excited at being left in charge.

'I'll manage.'

'Do you know how to get a fire going?' Tashelle asked in a way that suggested she doubted it.

'I was a Guide.'

Tashelle laughed. 'Of course you were.'

'And I was a Scout,' said Seth, making Daisy feel a lot better about Tashelle's petty jibe, designed to make her feel childish.

'Me too,' said Rich. 'Great times. Gave me an interest in surviving the great outdoors.'

'That's settled then,' Henry said, lifting his bowl to finish his soup. 'Right, with Daisy here, I'd like you to go to

Trench 3, Tashelle.'

'Fine by me.' Tashelle rubbed her hands.

Daisy was beginning to wish she hadn't agreed with Tashelle so willingly. Is that what she'd been angling for, taking her place with Seth?

'And Freja, you can help Rich at Trench 2. You've done enough filming for now. The others have their phones they can use for photos.'

'But Henry, that will leave you on your own at the monks' burial site.'

'I'll be fine. Sometimes I can get on better by myself.' He looked at his watch. 'Time to get back to the grindstone.'

Rich and Freja were the first to leave. Tashelle then headed off, beckoning Seth like a dog.

'I'll catch you up,' he said, taking. Daisy's hand. 'Are you sure you'll be all right here?'

'Absolutely, but thank you for your concern.'

'Ring if you're worried. If you can get a signal.'

'Unlikely, but I'll be OK.'

He kissed her and walked away, turned to wave, and then disappeared into the vegetation.

'Thank you for taking this on so willingly,' Henry said, pushing his arms through his backpack. 'I'll see you later.'

He tramped off eastwards to the Bronze Age site, and had soon disappeared behind the rock.

Daisy looked round, wondering what to do first. It was too early to light a fire, but she could build it up. She looked up at the grey clouds; not too dark today, but it might still rain.

What a shame they couldn't have stayed at Sealfarne Castle while they were here. It looked big enough to accommodate them all. Still, it might have looked too obvious that someone had been there, and Angus might not want the responsibility of guests.

She went to the trailer and lifted the tarpaulin, spotting the firewood straight away. She heaved out one of the bags, dropping it on the floor before she started lugging it to its destination.

Before she was halfway there, she heard a yell.

She stood up straight, spinning around, trying to work out where it had come from. It was a male voice. Most likely Henry, as he'd be the nearest. She hurried in the direction he'd gone, beyond the rock, and climbed the slight incline. There was a figure sprawled on the ground.

'Henry! What happened?'

He raised himself up on his hands, moaning.

'I don't know. Tripped over a rock, I think.'

'Don't move, hold on . . . ' Daisy carefully helped him up. 'Are you OK?'

'Just need a few seconds.'

'Were you attacked?'

There was a pause before Henry said, 'I don't think so. Just me being too hasty.'

'Come back to camp for a while.'

'No, no, dear, there's no need.' He struggled up to a standing position. 'No, I'll be fine. You get back to camp now and I'll see you at sunset.'

He walked away, a slight limp in evidence.

As she watched him disappear into the distance, the limp lessened then disappeared as he got into his stride. At least he wasn't badly hurt, and it had only been an accident.

Probably.

* * *

Seth and Tashelle had only walked a few yards before she said, 'There's a new bar opened near the campus. Fancy trying it one night after work?'

Even though they were in the open air, Seth felt the walls of Tashelle's fixation on him closing in around him. He replied as matter-of-factly as he could, 'Is that the one in the old bank that Rich was talking about?'

'That's the one. He went there with his girlfriend, said they'd done it up a treat. And they have a Happy Hour until seven on a Thursday.'

A gust of wind blew Tashelle's hair up, making her look like Medusa, surrounded by snakes. He laughed. Looking at her when she was angry could turn you to stone!

'What's funny?'

He daren't tell her. She'd never been able to laugh at herself. Daisy would probably have found it hilarious if it had been her, though she was too much the opposite — too self-critical.

'Nothing's funny. Wind took me by surprise. We could get a group together from the department and try the bar out one night.'

'You know what they say about three — or more in this case — being a crowd.'

He wasn't going to rise to it. 'That's the idea, isn't it? A nice crowd of us, having fun.'

They'd come to the monks' burial place, on the low levels of Stow Rise. Seth stopped to look out to sea.

'The waves are a bit choppy out there.'

Tashelle took a scrunchy out of her jacket pocket and attempted to pull her hair into a ponytail. She ended up tossing her head forward so her hair was over her face, then flinging it back in an attempt to get her hair in one place. She then gathered it up at the back and wrapped the scrunchy round it three times.

Seth waited until she finished before he replied. She always had to do everything with the utmost drama. 'They certainly are choppy. And the weather's deteriorating.'

'We'd better get a wiggle on then.' After a few steps she added, 'At least if we go to that bar dear little Daisy won't be coming. Not that they'd let her in. You have to be twenty-one. A teenager's a bit young for you, Seth, don't you think?'

Seth stopped long enough to say, 'She's twenty-four.'

'You said she was a first year.'

'Started uni late. A mature student, really.'

'Pff. Hardly mature!'

'Unlike you, ya mean?' He glanced back at her, eyebrows raised.

'What's that supposed to mean?'

'Look, let's get on with it. We might not have as long as we'd hoped with the weather.'

As they settled down in the trench by the partly dug bones, Tashelle said, 'Whoa! What have we got here? You didn't mention this at lunch.'

Seth's heart was heavy for a moment, missing Daisy here with him. 'There was hardly time, and Henry didn't seem in the mood.'

Tashelle brushed at the dirt. 'Do you think he has some idea what's going on? Could this have happened before, and that's why Sir James closed the dig?'

'But Henry's the only one from the original dig, so if someone was playing silly devils they're not here now. And Angus was only twelve, remember.'

'You're assuming it's a someone . . . '

Seth stopped scraping.

'What are you suggesting?'

'This place is creepy, the whole island, like there's . . . you know, a presence.'

Seth groaned. 'Oh, please! Ghosties and ghoulies and long-leggedy beasties?'

'And things that go bump in the night,' she finished. 'Not exactly, but you get a lot of stories of weird creatures, half seen but never caught.'

'I seem to remember you mocking Daisy with Big Foot when she referred to her assailant as 'it'. Anyway, I hope not, since we've left Daisy at camp on her own.' He was regretting that decision more and more.

'She's already been picked on. Have you noticed, nobody's been targeted twice?'

'Yet. Only three of you have been involved in an incident, so that's hardly a conclusive pattern. And if it's been planned, it's definitely a someone.'

'Oh, I don't know then. Perhaps it's the ghost of the Lady of Sealfarne, getting revenge for something.' Tashelle burrowed into the earth with the point of her trowel. 'The more I think about it, the less it makes sense. By the way, changing the subject somewhat, my sister's having a fancy dress party on New Year's Eve. Would you like to be my plus one?'

'I've told you, Tash, I've no intention of going down that route again. Once bitten, twice — '

'What's this?' Tashelle interrupted. 'Fingers? Wait.' She dug a little more. 'Yes! And what's this?' She brushed at the new items. 'Is that — ?'

Seth bent down to get a better look, shining the torch on the area. 'Good grief! Take a closer look. What do you think?'

She bent down as he got up, touching the newly found items delicately.

'Oh, man! That puts a whole new spin on it.'

'And then some.' Seth jumped up. 'We'd better get this packed up and get back to camp. We need to work out what we're going to do.'

'We should have another look at the other find,' Tashelle said. 'I have a feeling we missed something.'

Seth sighed. 'You're not kidding.'

★ ★ ★

Daisy had made the fire up and it was burning nicely now, the warmth compensating a little for her being here and not at Trench 3. The stew was simmering nicely in the pot hooked over the fire. She'd been tempted to go foraging for scurvy grass, be a bit adventurous, but the episodes of the last few days made her think twice.

The cloud cover overhead was slate grey, darker than earlier. Daisy shuddered despite the fire. It felt like a bad portent, even though she didn't believe in such things. She looked at her phone. Another hour before the group returned. Unless the weather got worse. The light was already pretty poor to be working by.

She rose and went to the boxes used to house the artefacts, stacked together by the trailer. The top one contained the bones of The Lady of Sealfarne. She carefully lifted it down and took it over to the flat rock near the fire. Halfway through the action of lifting the lid she froze. There was a rustling behind her, then a slight yipping sound, a bit like a dog.

She turned in slow motion, placing the lid back on the box as she did. If there was someone playing silly beggars, she was going to have the upper hand this time. Her gaze took in the area around her. What could she use to defend herself? A pot! She leant forward gradually, picking up the largest saucepan, doing a full three hundred and sixty degree turn with it. Nothing. The sound had stopped. No — there it was!

Feeling shaky she did another complete circle. Then she spotted something brown moving at the corner of her eye. She twisted, lifting the pan . . .

A fox.

She lowered the pan. It looked up at her, head to one side, cheeky as you like.

'You again, eh, Foxy? If it is you. I wonder how many of you there are on the island? I didn't know you made that yipping sound either.'

The fox held eye contact with her, frozen in mid-step. Did foxes attack humans? A guy on her course at uni claimed a couple of months back that he'd been chased by an urban fox in Ealing, of all places.

'If you're after the rabbit stew, you're out of luck, Foxy. Sorry.'

The fox lifted its head, blinking, as if to say, *You win some, you lose some,* before trotting off into the vegetation once more.

Daisy waited a few moments to make sure it didn't come back, then lifted the lid of the box once more. There was the skull she and Seth had found. She bit her bottom lip. She shouldn't really be interfering with it, but it was fascinating. Slowly lifting it out, she leaned forward to examine it. Amazing how well preserved it was compared to what they were sure were monks' remains. If this really was Bronze Age, it would be much older. The teeth were in fantastic condition — but then they didn't have sugar to rot them back then. She tilted it to examine the back teeth at the top.

Some grit seemed to have got into one of the molars. Hardly surprising, given that it was covered with earth. She peered closer, lifting a forefinger to touch it. Strange. She rubbed at it. It looked more like . . . no, it couldn't be . . .

There must be a proper torch somewhere. She went to the trailer and quickly found one, taking it back to the skull. Keeping it in the box this time, she tilted it up while shining the torch on it.

A cold shiver went through her. If that was what she thought it was, the whole dig had just turned several shades more treacherous.

10

Seth and Tashelle were the first to come back to camp, half-an-hour after Daisy's discovery. She could hear Tashelle's voice first, sounding anxious, then after a while the deeper, more soothing tones of Seth's voice. She was itching to tell someone what she'd found, yet dreading it at the same time. Judging by the last few days, Henry would do his nut! And it opened up a whole can of worms that Sir James MacKinnon was not going to like one little bit.

Was that why he'd closed the dig and buried it over? Oh boy, the next few days were going to be eventful, of that she had no doubt!

As soon as Tashelle and Seth appeared, Daisy blurted out, 'I've found something! If it's what I think it is it'll — '

'Never mind what you found,' Tashelle

shouted over her. 'What we've got here is dynamite!'

Daisy, far from backing down as Tashelle no doubt thought she would, shouted even louder, 'And so is what I've found. I think we're looking at murder!' She ended on a high note, in the way Tashelle often did, regretting the overplayed drama but wanting to get her point across.

Seth stepped in.

'OK, it could be what we've found is connected to what you found. You'd better show us.'

Leading them over to the box, she said, 'I wanted to have another look at the skull, I couldn't believe how perfectly preserved it seemed.'

'You shouldn't have been interfering with it,' Tashelle snarled.

'Well, its a good job I did, because we all missed something — something quite obvious, though it's position is slightly hidden, admittedly.' She took the lid off and tilted the skull back. Shining the torch on it, she said, 'So,

201

what do you think that is?'

'It's a dental filling,' Seth said. 'And does fit with what we've found.'

He placed the box he'd been carrying on the ground and lifted the lid.

Daisy put her hand to her mouth and gasped.

'Two rings on the third finger of her left hand — wedding and engagement rings — modern, too.'

Tashelle took the lid from Seth and covered the box back up. 'They are modern. But who the blazes could it be? The only woman on the island at the time of the dig was Lady MacKinnon, and she's alive and well with Sir James.'

Daisy clasped her hands together.

'No. Angus mentioned a tutor, Mary Armstrong.'

'You're right,' said Seth. 'Angus told us she didn't like the dig and tried to discourage him from visiting it.'

Tashelle pointed through the clear lid of the box. 'But that's a wedding ring. Angus didn't mention a husband. She could have been a widow.'

'Is it possible that whoever it is had a row with someone? Because after I found the filling, I had a closer look at the skull and found this . . .'

She went back to the box on the rock and carried it over gently. Seth lifted the skull to look, then showed Tashelle.

'That looks like a mighty big whack to the back of the head. Is it possible Angus lost his temper with her?'

Tashelle said, 'He was twelve years old!'

'And a big strapping lad even then, I wouldn't mind betting.'

'I can't see it somehow. It can't be long now before the rest of the team return.' Tashelle looked up to the sky. 'I'm surprised they're not back already with the early sunset.'

Daisy heard the distant sound of chatter.

'Here they are,' she said.

'I'm not looking forward to this,' Tashelle said.

Daisy had to agree.

★ ★ ★

Freja looked at Seth, Tashelle and Daisy in turn after she and the other two were asked to gather round the flat rock. 'What's this all about?'

'We've found something, and it's pretty major,' Tashelle blurted out.

Seth brought the boxes over. 'Let's get everyone's input first before we decide that. Henry, are you joining us?'

'What's going on?' he asked suspiciously.

First of all, Seth showed them the skull with the filling and the blow at the back of the skull.

Taking a deep breath, Freja stepped back. 'This place is cursed, I swear it is.'

Tashelle turned on her. 'Don't be so dramatic.'

'You can talk, Miss Drama Queen!'

'Yeah, maybe, but this isn't the time or place. The place may be weird, but certainly not cursed.'

Rich's face was grave.

'Whatever it is, it's a nightmare scenario.'

Tashelle brought out the arm and hand with the rings. 'We also found this, which might at least give up an identity. We think it's Angus's old tutor, Mary Armstrong. Henry, you must have met her. Was she a widow, or did she have a husband?'

Henry looked down at the arm. His face had turned ash grey as his lips parted slightly. Seth noticed he was breathing rapidly.

'Henry?' Seth tapped his shoulder. 'Can you shed any light on this?'

'It can't be Mary Armstrong,' he said, his voice shaking. 'How could you think it was?'

'She was the only other woman on the island at the time of the dig.'

'It can't be Mary Armstrong, Seth. She's in Edinburgh with James MacKinnon. She is the current Lady MacKinnon.'

The group looked round at each other, confused.

Seth was the first to recover from the announcement. 'You're clearly in possession of information we're all ignorant of. Would you like to share any more?'

'I wasn't purposely withholding information. It didn't seem to be of importance to the dig. I suggest we sit down. I certainly need to.'

They followed him to the seats round the fire, waiting for Henry to begin his story.

'James MacKinnon wrote to me about . . . I don't know, a month after we left the island, demanding to know where his wife Emma was. Apparently she'd run away and he assumed she was with me. I replied to him immediately to assure him I had not seen her. He wrote a few more times, claiming not to believe me. He even threatened to involve the police. I invited him to do so, as I was also keen to make sure Emma was safe.'

'And did he involve the police?' Seth asked.

'The police did visit me at one stage, after she'd been missing with no word for several months. They couldn't understand why she would have left without taking Angus. She was devoted to the boy. She lost several babies after he was born and was very protective of him.

'She'd apparently taken very few of

her possessions, in one small case, they seem to think. The police were satisfied she wasn't with me and also that I'd had nothing to do with her disappearance.'

Seth asked, 'Why would Sir James assume you had something to do with her disappearance?' He was pretty sure he already knew the answer.

'We fell in love. I think James had an inkling it had happened but did nothing. In the end she decided to stay with James for Angus's sake.

'Ben, another team member was interested in her, though I didn't think at the time she had any attraction for him. He left the department a few weeks after we returned from that dig. Just went home one evening and never returned. He phoned to say he was going travelling to find himself.' Henry coughed a brief, doleful laugh. 'I'd always thought that a ridiculous concept . . . as if you could lose yourself. Now I'm not so sure. I often wondered if Emma had been deceiving me as well, and went off with Ben.'

'Did the police speak to him?' Freja asked.

'I've no idea. About seven years later, I read in a local paper that Emma had never been located and so declared legally dead. James married Mary Armstrong, the tutor.' Henry closed his eyes and they creased as if he were in pain.

Seth patted him on the shoulder. 'I'm sorry. I know this is difficult, but could you tell us whether the rings might be Emma MacKinnon's?'

'Yes, they are. I'd recognise that engagement ring anywhere. Specially made, Emma told me. Two emeralds and a ruby. She said how it had become appropriate — that she and James were the two emeralds, and Angus was the ruby. She was sentimental. That was another reason she didn't want to leave James. He was a good man, she said, and he'd treated her like a queen.'

Tashelle shattered the sombre mood with, 'If by treating her like a queen you mean he executed her, like Henry VIII did Anne Boleyn and Katherine Howard, then yeah, I see what you mean.'

'Tashelle, for pity's sake,' Rich scolded. 'Have a little compassion for a change. Henry's just discovered the Lady of Sealfarne is the woman he loved.'

'That certainly turned out to be true.' Tashelle stood. 'I'm very sorry that our find turned out to be Lady Emma, but we now have a few urgent matters to attend to, Henry.'

'You're right. We need to decide what to do. To be honest, I suspected it was her the moment the first part of the — of Emma — was found, if for no other reason than the presence of the Bronze Age bracelet.'

'How come?' Seth prompted.

'Did you not think it odd that there were no other similar pieces of jewellery with it?'

'It occurred to me briefly, but if doing this job has taught me anything, it's expect the unexpected.'

'The truth is, it didn't come from here at all. We never found any jewellery at the Bronze Age trench on the first dig — only pots. But Emma admired the workmanship and design of the period greatly, from photos she'd seen in books. She was a very keen amateur archaeologist. The bracelet was one of many we found at a dig in Cumbria. I know it was bad of me, but I didn't think anyone would miss it, so I gave it to her.'

'Oh, Henry,' Freja said, as if talking to a child. 'Do you think Sir James found it and realised something was going on? Then used the closing of the dig as a means of hiding the body?'

'But James closed the dig before Emma went missing. She was still here when we left.'

'Then he planned it in advance. However you look at it, he must have had something to do with it. He buried the body in one of the trenches to conceal her, then had the digger cover her with even more soil, guaranteeing no one would find her. No wonder he didn't want you coming back here. And

he tried to frame you for her disappearance.'

Henry lowered his head into his hands.
'What have I done?'

'What you've done is reveal the
truth,' Seth said. 'We need to get the
police involved now.'

Henry shook his head. 'We should
re-bury her, leave her in peace. What's
the point of raking it all up after all
these years?'

Seth stood up, lifting his phone from
his pocket and holding it up to try and
get a signal. 'You know we can't do that,
Henry.' A thought occurred to him. 'Why
did you want to come back? Surely the
memories would be too upsetting.'

Henry raised his tear-stained face. 'I
wasn't convinced she was really dead,
since they'd never found a body. I wrote
several times to James, imploring him
to let the team return, but to no avail.
When Angus wrote to me I had this
mad idea that I could find out where
Emma had gone, that maybe Angus had
contact with her and she'd come here

to see me while James was away. I realised quite quickly it had all been a mistake, that the past should be left in the past.'

'If we all thought like that, we'd be out of a job,' Tashelle pointed out. 'The past is our business.'

Seth walked round the camp. 'It's no good. I'm not getting any kind of signal. Anyone else?'

Tashelle tried the same with her phone. 'Nothing here either. What are we going to do? The boat's not even due to pick us up until the thirty-first. And Angus's boat is too small to get everything on.'

'May I make a suggestion?' Daisy put her hand part way up. 'I think we should go to the castle. Angus might have a landline there.'

Rich was now walking round with his phone aloft. 'I dunno. Do we want to let Angus in on this? What if he already knows something?'

'If he does, that might be why he asked you to come out here,' Daisy said. 'Perhaps he couldn't just go to the police in case it turned into a wild goose chase and he got on the wrong side of his father. The police might not have dug up as much as we have on the word of someone who was twelve at the time.'

Seth took a decision since Henry was evidently incapable of doing so at that moment.

'Daisy's right. We're going to have to let Angus know. The most difficult bit is going to be telling him we've found his mother. I don't relish that.'

Henry heaved himself up with some effort. He rubbed his hands across his face. 'I'll do that.'

Freja placed a lid on one of the boxes. 'We'd better leave these here. We can't lug everything across the island. If we put them in the trailer and tie the tarpaulin on tight . . . that's a point. We still don't know who or what caused these accidents.'

Tashelle lifted her hands, still marked with spots of blood where the gorse spines had entered. 'If I ever get my hands on them . . .'

Rich gently rubbed the scrape on his face, which was crimson and purple. 'Get in line!'

Daisy stopped in the middle of picking up the other box. 'And Henry fell over after lunch.'

'It was nothing, no need to cause a fuss. I probably just tripped, clumsy clogs that I am.'

The professor had never been clumsy in his life. Seth could tell there was more to it, but Henry was in no state for any more cross-examination.

★ ★ ★

It was getting dark before they even got half way across the island. Seth, Rich and Tashelle shone their torches on the path, though it was still hard to make out stray rocks and boulders. A couple of them had stumbled along the way, including Henry. He'd been otherwise silent, not joining in with the conversation on the situation.

Daisy couldn't help thinking they should have waited until morning. On the other hand, she didn't relish sharing a camp with the late Lady Emma. The presence of the monks' bones hadn't bothered her at all, but this was too personal.

When there was a lull in the conversation, she said, 'Have you noticed Angus hasn't been over to see how we're getting on the last two days? He seemed really keen at first. I hope he's OK.'

Freja humphed. 'Unless he's got other reasons for keeping a low profile. He's still top of my list for all the trouble.'

Daisy had to agree it didn't look good. This isle was the furthest out of the Farne Islands. There weren't even any commercial trips to see the wildlife this time of year, and none of their group seemed to have a motive. Unless . . .

Tashelle came to a standstill, shining her torch back on the others, causing them all to cover their eyes. 'I think we're on a fool's errand here. Even if we get hold of the police, they're not going to come out here now.'

Seth walked past her. 'But at least they can come out first thing in the morning.'

Tashelle hung back, before catching them up with an impatient sigh. 'I hope that food Daisy's cooked isn't ruined by the time we get back.'

'I put it on a higher hook,' Rich said. 'It'll be fine. Let's get on with this.'

Twenty minutes later they were outside Sealfarne Castle, its tall, rugged stone structure ominous in the light of the three torches. The yew trees surrounding it swayed their branches in the whistling breeze.

Daisy surveyed all the windows, eight of them on the west side, all at different levels. She still reckoned there were three floors.

'I can't see any lights on,' she said.

'I'll have a look on the other side,' Seth said.

Daisy hurried on after him. 'Not on your own, you're not. It's not safe.'

The east side, which in the daylight overlooked the jetty, also displayed no lights at the windows.

Daisy took hold of Seth's arm. 'It's a bit early for going to bed, isn't it?'

'Maybe he's not even here. He could have taken his motor boat back to the mainland.'

'There's one way to find out.'

They trod carefully until they reached the wooden planks of the path that led down to the jetty. It was easier to walk here. Seth shone his torch towards the water, sweeping the beam around to take in the whole jetty area.

'There it is,' he said. 'So unless he's hired a boat to take him back, he's still here.'

Daisy snuggled in closer to Seth.

'Let's get back to the others.'

As they turned back they heard hammering on the tall, wooden double front doors, the dull thud filling the darkness.

It was Rich, the rest of the party gathered around him. He stopped knocking after several attempts. 'It's no good. He either isn't in there, or he's not answering. Find anything else?'

'The boat's still there,' Seth said.

217

Tashelle suddenly swung an arm out, attempting to grab at Freja's camera. 'For crying out loud, stop filming us! This is nothing to do with the dig.'

Freja jumped backwards, putting the camera behind her back. 'Don't you touch me!'

'I swear if you get that thing out once more I'll lay you flat!'

'You and whose army?' Freja scoffed.

'That's enough, both of you!' yelled Seth. 'But Freja, please, filming this is not appropriate.'

It seemed to Daisy that he'd well and truly taken charge of the expedition, as Henry stood there limply, looking up at the house.

Freja wrapped her arms around herself, running on the spot. 'I don't like this. It can't be coincidence . . . the attacks, the body, Angus missing. Why don't we break into the house and stay there for the night? It'd be better than being unprotected in tents. We've got to do something otherwise we'll all come a-cropper.'

'Pull yourself together,' Seth said. 'We can't just break into someone's home. Besides, look at the size of the doors. I wouldn't like to try ramming them open, would you?'

Henry finally spoke. 'You'll be fine, Freja. We all will. Nothing's going to happen to us.'

'But there's still someone out there.'

'Well, it's not going to bother us tonight.'

'How can you be so sure?'

Henry hesitated. 'Because it never does when we're all together, does it?'

'I suppose not.' Freja yawned. 'In that case, let's get back to our supper. I'm starving.'

★ ★ ★

By the time they got back to camp the wind had whipped up more fiercely. The fabric of the tents was flapping and vibrating, but they were still holding fast. The fire had gone out. Rich tapped the pot hanging over the dying embers.

'It's still hot,' he said. 'I'll build another fire but I'm not sure how it'll fare in this wind. Maybe with us sitting around it'll shelter it a bit.'

He went to work as Daisy handed round the stew in the light of the three torches, set on the rock to shine at them. She made sure there was plenty left for Rich. If he couldn't get the fire going the only alternative was to sit in their tents in their sleeping bags. It would be a long night if they had to do that.

Rich managed to get the fire going and showed much appreciation for the stew once he'd finished.

Freja, who finished first, was fiddling around in her large photography bag, putting the camera she'd been using today away. She got her phone out of her pocket, staring at the screen and running her finger along it every few seconds.

'You won't get any signal here, if that's what you're looking for,' Tashelle said.

'I'm not expecting any. I'm reading a book I downloaded.'

Tashelle grunted. 'I tried my phone several times along the path, and at the house. Nothing. Imagine living in a place with no mobile signal. Now that is a nightmare scenario.'

'I could get used to it,' Seth said. 'I tried my phone too and had no luck.'

When everyone had finished the meal, the five archaeologists headed to the trailer, to check all was as it should be and make sure the boxes were safe should there be a storm.

A *storm*, thought Daisy, remaining by the wavering fireside. That would heap a whole new type of misery on this affair. She thought about Callie, Bea, Dave and Toby, curled up watching a soppy Christmas film, or playing one of the new games Cal had bought, slowly getting sozzled in a nice warm house. At home, her aunt, uncles and their families would be arriving with gifts of wine and chocolate, as was their habit. There'd be games and laughter in a cosy house.

Oh, but neither of those scenarios

would be much of a tale to relate to her housemates or her uni friends; she could dine out on this for months! Who'd have thought it? Mousy little Daisy Morgan on an island full of intrigue.

She looked over to where the others were leaning over the finds. She caught the odd word about where the artefacts would need to go, and then about whether the police would take everything away with them. This dragged her back to reality. Intriguing it might be, but not at all nice for those originally involved.

She rose to gather up the bowls, spotting something shimmering by the third tent. A notebook, the glittery pattern of which was caught by the torches. She picked it up. Must belong to one of the others. She hadn't noticed any of them with one like this. Opening it, she looked on the inside cover to see if there was a clue to its owner. Nothing. Meaning to glance only briefly at the first page, she was captured by the content. It was an outline for a TV show about a group of archaeologists caught in the middle of nowhere, and how they all turned on each other as things went wrong. Written near the top was *Working title: When Digs Get Dirty*.

She skimmed the pages, reading notes about things that had happened and people's reactions. It obviously belonged to Freja. Suddenly Daisy's own name caught her eye. She knew she should shut the book, but read on . . . *Daisy, the too-good-to-be-true sickly sweet girlfriend (possibly) of the lovely Seth. Would be good if the worm turned and we discovered she's a nasty piece of work. Or if Tash swung for her! Great TV!*

Daisy felt sick. Is that what people thought — that she was putting on a mask, pretending to be nice when she wasn't? She'd always tried to see the best in people, to get along with everyone. She'd love to have the confidence Freja and Tashelle possessed. What should she do about the book? Best to hide it for now and think about it. She quickly slipped it into her tent. She could always leave it somewhere for Freja to find tomorrow.

When they all returned to their seats by the fire, Rich said, 'Tea, anyone?'

Henry rose. 'I think I have something people might appreciate more.' He went to his tent, coming back with a bottle of whisky. 'Single malt. For emergencies. Now maybe that time.'

Daisy wasn't overly fond of whisky, but since everyone else seemed keen she held out her tin mug too. After what she'd just found, she could do with it. She shuddered as the whisky went down, but it provided a warm glow. That and Seth next to her, snuggling up close, made her feel a whole lot better.

She felt the first wet drops on her head as she drained her mug. 'Is that rain?'

'I didn't feel anything — ' Tashelle started. 'Oh, yeah . . . I can feel it now.'

It soon progressed from spitting to drizzling.

'We'd better put the chairs under cover, then go to our tents before it gets worse,' Rich advised. 'No point going to bed wet if we can help it. You didn't predict this rain, Prof.'

'No.' In the background came a growl of thunder. 'Could be a cold front coming in.'

'You know, sometimes I hate this job,' Tashelle complained through gritted teeth.

They all ran to their tents, a symphony of zips accompanying another rumble.

Daisy slipped off her boots before checking her phone. Five past six. Just over thirteen hours until it was time to get up. She plugged her phone into the portable charger she'd brought. There couldn't be much above one charge left now. They must all be in the same position. She might as well turn it off and save the battery.

She pulled out the small torch Callie had loaned her, along with a novel. This should keep her busy for a while, unless the torch ran out of charge. She slipped off her coat, jumper and jeans, but kept the rest of her clothes on before slipping into the sleeping bag. It ws a shame she wasn't squashed up next to Seth tonight — at least she'd have had someone to talk to.

She opened the book and slipped the makeshift bookmark out. She hadn't even read a full page before she fell asleep.

★ ★ ★

Daisy didn't have any idea how many hours sleep she actually got in the end, with the lightning flashing nearby, the intermittent rumble of thunder, and the odd shower beating on the tent. When she woke the rain had stopped, but it was still dark. She shone her small torch around, feeling the covers with her other hand. It all seemed dry. That was something, at least.

Being awake much of the night had given Daisy time to think about her life — where it was going. All the strands of her thoughts had led back to the same conclusion. *Archaeology*. That's what she'd really like to do.

What would her parents say if she told them she wanted to swap, start again? What if she couldn't get a place at Northumbria University? Did she want to do archaeology only because of Seth? It was certainly a factor. She'd only known him eight days. Would he want a holiday fling tipping up at his university? What if the relationship went horribly wrong? The whole thing was crazy!

She turned her phone on. Nearly eight o'clock. Time to shake a leg. Goodness knew what it would be like outside.

She dressed quickly and unzipped the tent, peering out. The rain had stopped, but the sky, with only a hint of light in the east, was still overcast. People were already huddled round the fire — except there wasn't one.

Daisy walked on her knees out of the tent and zipped it back up. 'Morning.'

There was a low rumble of replies. Only Seth called brightly, 'Morning, Daisy.'

When she reached the seating area she noticed they were all gathered apart from Freja — as usual. She sat in the space next to Tashelle, who was next to the flat rock.

'I'm afraid it's cold breakfast today,' Seth informed her. 'Crispbread, butter and jam.'

Rich, on the other side of the rock, handed her a plate with two crispbreads. 'The ground's too wet to get the fire going for porridge. Help yourself.' He indicated the flat rock where the butter and two pots of jam were laid out.

Daisy smiled. 'Thanks. I'm good with crispbread and jam.' In truth she'd have loved a bowl of hot porridge, but there was no point in saying that.

'Of course you are,' Tashelle muttered. Louder she said, 'What do you want us to do today, Henry? I presume we're not going back to the trenches to dig . . . Henry?'

He took a while to come to, looking around as if he wasn't sure who'd spoken.

'Henry, what are we doing?' she repeated.

'Oh, um . . . well, not digging. I think

we can safely say that will have to be put on hold. Which means forever, of course, given the circumstances.'

Freja appeared in her trademark early morning kaftan, taking a seat between Daisy and Henry.

'Good morning, everyone.'

Tashelle glared at her. 'No it isn't. And aren't you cold in that thing?'

'Nope. Got thermals on underneath. That thunder and lightning didn't let up much last night, did it? I love storms, but boy, they're quite scary when you're in a tent.'

'For crying out loud!' shouted Tashelle. 'This isn't the time for your cheerful banter.'

'It's better than being a misery guts like you. So Henry, I just heard you tell everyone what we're *not* doing, but what *are* we doing?'

'Staying put. We can take the time to finish any notes and records. Unless someone can get a signal on their phone, I don't see us getting off the island any time soon.'

'How did you think we were going to get off before, when you were so keen to?' Rich asked.

'I assumed we'd use a land line at Angus's. I just wanted to protect my team.'

Rich picked up a crispbread, then put it down again. 'Or yourself. I was willing to give you the benefit of the doubt before, but now, with all that's happened, I'm not so sure. Though I can't work out how the two things are linked, but I'm darned sure they are.'

Tashelle jumped up. 'If you've got something to say, Rich, just spill it, will you? What links are you yabbering on about?'

'All right, all right, keep your hair on. Two days ago I found a folder behind a chair. You remember, Tash, don't you?'

'Yes, they were trench records, weren't they?'

'That's right,' Seth added.

'Department papers. I was flicking through, to see who they belonged to, and came across a letter to Henry. A few key words caught my eye.'

Henry threw his empty tin plate towards where the fire should have been. 'You have no right to look through my private papers.'

'It's a good job I did, because I found a letter which implies — '

Henry wagged a forefinger in Rich's direction. 'I'm warning you. I don't need everyone knowing my business.'

'And what are you going to do about it, eh?'

'I can sack you.' Henry looked away, mouth pinched, arms crossed.

Daisy, dying to know what was in the letter, looked over at Seth on the opposite side, catching his eye. She raised her eyebrows in question. He lifted his shoulders slightly, which indicated to her he didn't know either.

'Oh really,' Rich said. 'And how will you do that if you're working at another university?'

When Henry didn't reply, Seth said calmly, 'Would you care to explain, Henry? I thought you were retiring.'

'Not that it's anyone's business, but

231

I said I'd do a favour for Professor Maggie Perryman at Torquay University, just for one dig on Exmoor. She's short of good archaeologists. Maggie and I have known each other for years, since we were students together.'

Rich stood up, shouting, 'You're a liar! You wanted to take some of the work we've been doing somewhere else. Maybe this dig too. Why not say something otherwise? By your own admission you stole a Bronze Age bracelet to give to your lover. What else would you stoop to?'

Henry got to his feet, facing Rich, his face just inches from his.

'How dare you! Emma was not my lover, but someone I was in love with. Nothing ever happened between us. We acted decently.'

Seth ducked from under the two men, pulling himself up to his full height.

'Lady MacKinnon apart, Henry, Rich has a point. Why not say you were helping Professor Perryman out? Why keep that under wraps?'

'I didn't want to say anything until it

was settled. I'm a private person, you know that, Seth.'

'Private or secretive?' Tashelle asked. 'In my experience people use 'private' to be deceptive.'

Henry's eyes swept round the group. 'Why would I bring you all here in the first place if I intended taking the finding to another university?'

'So you have something to offer,' Rich said. 'And because it's the only opportunity you have to come here.'

'This dig was last minute, you know that. Angus contacted me just before Christmas. Talk sense, man!'

Rich started to turn away, only to swing back.

'Perhaps that's why you engineered all the mishaps while we've been here. You were hoping we'd all flee and you'd have an excuse to bring another team in.'

Henry thumped himself back in his seat, not looking at Rich as he said, 'Do you think I'd do all that merely to take a dig to another university?'

Seth indicated to Rich to sit down.

'We've gone as far as we can with that accusation.'

Freja got up to help herself to water from the large bottle. 'My money's on Angus being responsible for the mishaps, as Rich calls them.'

Daisy had thought long and hard about this during the night, when she wasn't considering her own future. She piped up with, 'But it still comes down to why Angus would ask you here in the first place if he wanted to compromise the dig.'

Rich clicked his fingers. 'Exactly! So that still leaves Henry with the most to gain.'

'And you don't?' Tashelle said. 'It could just as easily be some kind of twisted revenge on your part, to get back at Henry for not promoting you.'

Rich pointed to his face. 'I was attacked, too.'

Tashelle tipped her head to one side.

'But were you? You could have climbed down the cliff and pretended to be barely holding on.'

'Freja pulled me up.' He looked in her direction. 'Did I look as if I could have pulled myself up?'

Freja blew a sigh upwards, dislodging her fringe. 'Probably not. It's pretty sheer there.'

'No,' Rich said. 'More likely you're accusing me, Tashelle, because you're the one responsible due to your jealousy of Daisy. You want to take it out on all of us, because that's the kind of spoilt brat you are.'

Tashelle pouted her lips and placed her hands on her hips, looking for all the world like the spoilt brat Rich was accusing her of being.

'You were the closest when Daisy was set on in the tent.'

'Yeah, but I was at the powder room. And I was pushed into the gorse.' She pointed to her spoilt jeans, still with the blood spots.

Seth moved out of the circle to look at them all. 'This has descended into a ridiculous tit-for-tat.'

'I agree,' Freja said. 'Because we've

all missed the obvious. We've all been on digs together before — apart from the newbie.' She pointed to Daisy. 'She wormed her way in and is suddenly interested in archaeology.'

Daisy had wondered when someone would get round to this accusation.

'How would I have arranged a meeting with Seth when I didn't even know him, let alone know he was going to turn up at our place? And he didn't know he was coming here until the phone call just before Christmas.'

She thought back to her first meeting with Seth at the bar, spilling beer down his lovely suit, discovering he was a friend of Callie's and Dave's. Then she remembered something else . . . the notebook she found last night, still concealed in her tent. She didn't like the atmosphere caused by the accusations and counter-accusations, but the book might clear up a few things. Besides, she was still sorely miffed by Freja's comments in the notebook, and those very comments might reveal she was blaming

Daisy just for show.

And to think Freja had been so friendly. As least she knew where she was with Tashelle.

'No, I've nothing to do with this sorry situation, but I did find something last night that could shed some light on it . . .'

She went to her tent and returned a moment later with the notebook. When Freja spotted it, she leapt over to retrieve it.

'Give me that back you thieving toe-rag! You're as bad as Rich!'

Daisy ran backwards and Seth jumped in between them, shielding her from Freja.

'I didn't steal it. Like Rich, I found it on the ground last night and looked inside only to find out whose it was. I assumed it was field notes. But when I caught sight of the first page I was disgusted by what I saw.'

'I know how you feel,' Rich piped up.

'Give it back!' Freja lunged forward again. This time Rich joined Seth in keeping her away from Daisy, pulling her back into the circle.

Daisy read out the first page, producing several angry cries from the group. Henry remained resolutely quiet but his expression darkened. She then picked random passages from different parts of the notebook, at the same time feeling guilty that she was enjoying Freja's discomfort. But really, it served her right!

When Daisy closed the book, Tashelle said accusingly, '*When Digs Get Dirty*? That's low, even for you, Freja.'

Freja shook Rich's hand off her arm.

'Yah, guilty as charged. That's the trouble in the TV reality game, you have to find something each time that outdoes what you did before. But, despite what it looks like, I did not have anything to do with the attacks or the ransacking of the camp. I promise you that. One of my camera lenses was broken in that incident. My cameras are my babies.'

Henry heaved himself up.

'Well, that concludes the evidence for the defence.'

Freja was the only one to laugh and it was clear by Henry's disapproving glance that he had not meant it as a joke.

'I'd like you all to do as I suggested earlier,' Henry continued. 'Catch up with notes. I want no arguments while I'm away. I'm going to look for Angus. At lunchtime, we'll talk again about what to do. I'll see you all later.'

Henry picked up his rucksack and tramped off in the direction of the house.

Daisy counted in her head. It was Friday the twenty-eighth today. If they couldn't contact anyone, they'd be here three more days.

It would be a very long three days.

11

The atmosphere at camp was strained. The four archaeologists remaining had their heads down, catching up with the record-keeping the dark evenings had made it hard to complete.

Daisy felt at a loss, trying to read the book Seth had given her but finding it hard to concentrate with all that had happened.

Seth had not said much, sitting at the opposite side of camp with a box of artefacts next to him, head down, writing copious notes. Every now and then he'd stop, place the top of his ballpoint between his teeth, eyes screwed up in thought. Then he'd be off again.

After nearly an hour, and only four pages read that she couldn't even remember, Daisy stuck the book back in her tent. The clouds had cleared since early that morning, and the sun had a chance to peep through now and then. It was so changeable here.

She rose and walked over to Seth.

'I think I'll go for a walk while it's reasonable. Unless there's anything I can do here.'

'Not at the moment. Are you sure you want to go off on your own?'

'Despite what people think, I'm a big girl now.'

Seth raised a small smile.

'I don't doubt it. Take a map with you, though.'

She headed to the box with the maps and helped herself to one.

'Perhaps later I could make some lunch? And who knows, I might get a signal while I'm gone.'

'Good luck with that,' Tashelle said, laying her pen down on her paper to untie and re-tie her ponytail. 'Wish I could escape for a while. Be careful out there.'

Tashelle's words were delivered in good spirit and, for a change, Daisy found no underlying spite in them.

'I might see what's on the beach for lunch,' were her parting words.

She took the route towards the path that led to the beach where Seth had found the shellfish. If the ground had dried out a bit, and it seemed likely with the combination of breeze and sun, she could light a fire and cook them the way he had. Her mouth watered at the idea as she tramped through dandelions and dock leaves.

When she reached the crossing of the paths she had second thoughts. Ahead was How Rise, the highest of the hillocks on the island. If she could get a signal anywhere it would be there.

The path passed close by Trench 1, where she'd worked with Seth. How Rise, sloping only gently upwards, should have been little more trouble to climb than a wheelchair ramp, but the lack of a path through the disorganised but abundant plants, along with the odd boulder, made it more difficult. Nearing the top, the vegetation thinned, then disappeared. Now the problem was keeping her feet from sliding on the smooth rock surface.

When she reached the top, she turned to take it all in. She could just make out the castle in the distance, so that must be roughly north. Further out, the other islands and the mainland were shrouded in mist. It would have been beautiful if it hadn't made her feel they were cut off from the rest of the world.

She pulled her phone out of her jacket pocket. Nothing. She lifted it up, where, for a split second, it seemed to have one bar. She stepped slowly across the flat peak, all the while keeping her eyes on her mobile. There it was again. Moving it this way and that, she finally found a spot where she had two bars.

Would that be enough? Who should she call? She had no idea what the number of the police in either Seahouses or Bamburgh was. If she rang 999, what could she say the emergency was? A woman was murdered here thirty years ago?

She looked at her phone as if it could

give her the answer. Then one did come to her. Directory enquiries. She'd never rung it before but there was a first time for everything. She would ask for the police in Berwick, which would doubtless have a bigger station. Having obtained the number, she rang it, taking a deep breath as she explained what had happened.

After the phone call was over, Daisy sat on the hilltop, a wave of relief making her feel much better about the situation. At least someone in the outside world knew what had happened, even if they couldn't get here just yet.

Perhaps starting with the historical murder hadn't been the best way to give her account, the policewoman on the other end naturally assuming she meant it had happened recently. Eventually she'd got the order of the events right and PC Turnbull, as she'd been called, had understood the dilemma. The news she'd been given, that the weather was due to get worse before it got better, hadn't been any comfort. It would be a while before they were able to send anyone out.

Daisy looked around, only now noticing that a fog had drawn in during her long telephone conversation. Which way had she come up?

There were no landmarks visible now. She'd have to trust her instinct. What could she use to guide her? There was that pretty yellow lichen on the rocks before she reached the summit. She walked to her left, picking some out on the rock. But walking in the opposite direction she saw it was on the rock there, too.

Whichever way she went down, she'd get somewhere. It was only a small island. If she got to the beach she'd know she'd walked southeast. Then she could look for the path and work out the direction to camp.

But what if the beach wasn't one of the two near the Bronze Age trench, but the one on the north-east side?

'Just walk. I'll work it out when I get there,' she told herself firmly, creeping slowly and carefully down. She made her way past rock to vegetation. Unless she stumbled across the beach, she'd never find it.

So much for collecting shellfish for lunch.

There were a lot of gorse bushes here, many of them in flower. She tried to picture her walks to Trench 1 with Seth. It was no good. There were gorse bushes all over the place. She could still be anywhere on that quarter of the island.

The fog grew thicker the lower she got, not allowing her to see any further than a metre in front. She took each step slowly, peering as best she could at what was ahead.

Trying to take a step forward, she suddenly found herself pulled back.

Her sleeve was caught on gorse spines. She tried untangling it, but when it wouldn't budge she wrenched her arm away. As a result she stumbled a couple of steps backwards. Cursing her stupidity, she waited for the hard ground or spiky bushes to end her fall, but neither did.

It was then she remembered. The cliffs.

12

It was a while before Seth was aware of a new chill in the air, making the area colder than it had been. He'd been engrossed in his work, not noticing until he looked up that Tashelle had a shawl draped over her jacket.

'I wouldn't fancy exploring the island in this,' she said, looking up.

A spike of fear jabbed at him as he thought of Daisy alone, walking almost blind into unknown hazards. 'I should go and look for her.'

'How? It's not as if you could even see where you're going.'

She wasn't wrong, but it didn't feel right, him sitting here working, while she could be in danger.

Tashelle pulled the shawl tighter around herself.

'Henry's out there, too.'

'He's used to all conditions. Daisy

won't know what to do. What an idiot I am, letting her go.'

'You her keeper, then?' Tashelle snapped.

'Of course not, but I'll never forgive myself if she gets hurt.' He stood and put his notes down.

'You're not going to look for her, are you?'

'Like you said, how? But sitting here writing notes, as if nothing had happened, doesn't seem a good option either.'

At that moment Henry appeared through the mist into the camp.

'Henry! How did you get back in this?'

'I wasn't far away when it descended. I used my compass.'

Seth groaned. 'A compass. I should have given Daisy one. A map's little use in this weather unless you have one.'

Henry looked round. 'Where is Daisy?'

'She went for a walk before the fog.'

'Did she say where she was going?'

Seth thought back. 'She mentioned the possibility of the beach.'

'Which one?'

'I assume Eigbech, the nearest to where we were working, but she didn't say.'

'She seems like a sensible young woman. I'm sure she'll stay put until it lifts. That would be the safest option.'

And the coldest, thought Seth. *Especially with this new chill.*

Freja wandered over from near the trailer, where she'd taken her seat to work away from the others. 'Serves her right if she gets lost, trying to pin those attacks on me.'

Tashelle clucked her tongue in disgust. 'You really are a prize witch, aren't you? It's one thing being resentful, but wishing harm on someone?'

'Just saying it like it is. She's not one of us.'

'She's more one of us than *you* are, coming here with your agenda. You'd have made total fools of us on one of your stupid reality TV shows if Daisy hadn't found your notebook.'

'Who says I still can't?' Freja stuck her head up in the air as if in victory.

'The fact I removed the SD cards from your cameras and bags while you were at the powder room and hid them?'

'You did what?' Freja was red in the face, wringing her hands. 'Give them back!'

Henry lifted a hand, palm outward. 'I think not. I thought you came here to help me, Freja. You've let me down badly.'

'Oh, puh-lease, don't lay that disappointed rubbish on me. You'll not get away with this.'

Freja went back to sitting in her seat by the trailer. Henry followed her over, wagging his finger and shaking his head. Seth could hear the odd words, like 'trusted' and 'in good faith'.

Tashelle broke his concentration with, 'This mist appears to be lifting. The sun's even trying to shine through. Don't worry, Seth, I'm sure Daisy will be OK. She seems quite sensible.'

What just happened there? Seth looked curiously at Tashelle as she went back to her papers and started writing again.

If Daisy was heading to a beach it did make sense that it would be the one nearest the dig, where they'd diverted to one day on the way to Trench 1. She'd surely stick to the path.

He hurried to his tent to fetch his rucksack, checking his compass and map were still in there.

'I'm going to look for Daisy,' he announced.

'It's up to you,' Henry said. 'I dare say you wouldn't take any notice of me trying to talk you out of it.'

'You're right, I wouldn't.'

'Good luck.' Tashelle lifted her hand to wave as he walked from the camp.

Heading east he quickly found the track. He checked his compass again. Yes, a left turn should bring him to the track crossover point. When he reached it, he stopped. Straight on to the dig, and turn right there to go to the beach, or go right here, on the track? He'd get to different ends of the beach. He decided to go straight to the beach first, then walk along.

The mist was slowly evaporating as he stepped carefully along the way. He reached the beach in a couple of minutes.

The sand was damp, making its usual golden hue more of a dirty yellow. He could now see around twenty feet in front of him. It could be that the mist had lifted enough to help Daisy find her way back to camp. He could only hope.

Seth made his way along the beach and found the small path that led up to the dig, and still no Daisy. Could she have gone to the other nearby beach, or up How Rise? The second option wouldn't be clever in the mist, but then it wasn't misty when she set off. He stopped a moment while the feeling of helplessness overwhelmed him. He had to be positive, carry on.

From the dig he made his way north to the path, turning right and going towards the next beach.

He'd almost reached the end of that path, spying the beach just ahead, when he heard something. Grey seals calling? Whatever it was had stopped.

He took a few steps forward and was brought to a halt once more. There it was again. He almost fancied he heard the word *Help!* He stood dead still. Yes, there it was again, he was sure.

'Daisy? Daisy! Are you here?'

'Seth? Seth!'

It was coming from inland. The relief surrounded him like a warm blanket. He started off through the plant life. 'Daisy, keep talking, as loudly as you can. I'll find you.'

'Seth!' The voice was now louder. 'My foot's trapped in something . . . a rabbit hole, I think.'

'OK, I'm coming. Keep talking. Do you know which direction you were coming from?'

'I was coming down How Rise. The mist came and I didn't know which direction I'd gone.'

He pushed the overgrown vegetation

away as he stepped purposefully towards Daisy's voice.

'You came down near Eigbech beach. I was at the path when I heard you. Are you OK?'

There was no time for her to reply as Seth spotted her through the haze, and he quickened his step.

'Daisy!'

She was facing down the hill on a bed of scurvy grass and was slumped to one side. Sure enough, her foot was wedged in a hole up to her ankle.

'Oh Seth, thank goodness! I'm so sorry. Did you come to find me?'

'I couldn't leave you out in this.'

'But you might have got lost, too.' He could tell she was on the verge of tears.

'Never mind that. Let's have a look.' He hunkered down. 'I think this might be a puffin hole rather than a rabbit hole. Look, there are a few around here. Does your foot hurt?'

'Not really. But it did when I tried to get it out. And I'm at quite an awkward angle.'

'Were you set upon?'

'No, I'm absolutely sure I wasn't. I got caught on the gorse, pulled too hard and lost my footing. That's it. In a way I'm thankful. When I didn't hit the ground I felt sure I'd gone over a cliff. I forgot I was going downhill.'

'Right, let's get you on your front, then your foot'll be in a better position to come out.'

After rotating her so she was facing down, he pulled his trowel out of his bag, digging around her foot. Gradually easing it out, he said, 'There you go. How do you feel now?'

She sat up and waggled her foot. 'It's a bit sore but it's OK. Thank you, Seth.'

He helped her stand, and when they'd established she was able to take the weight on her foot, she hugged him. They stayed like that for long seconds, clinging on, until he pulled away and kissed her.

'That's better,' she said when she came up for air. 'Can we get back to camp now? Oh, I've just realised I was supposed to be doing lunch! I'm sorry.'

'Don't be daft. Someone will sort something out. Might be down to the tinned stuff now.'

'I don't care, I'm starving.'

She took a few tentative steps, with Seth clutching her arm. 'I'm OK to walk.'

'I'm going to hold onto you anyway.' He let go of her arm and took her hand instead.

'That's nice. While we're walking back . . . '

She was about to say *I've got something I want to discuss with you. An idea I've had.* But now, just thinking about it made her stomach roil.

'While we're walking back, what?'

'You can tell me what's been happening at camp while I've been gone. If anything.'

Chicken! Guilty as charged. She *would* run the idea past him. Just not yet.

★   ★   ★

The first person Daisy saw back at camp was Tashelle, running towards them once she spotted them. Behind her Rich was at the camp fire and Henry was sitting writing notes. They both looked up and waved.

'You found her,' Tashelle called, in a breathy voice. 'Thank goodness! Are you OK?'

Daisy wasn't sure what to do with this concern of Tashelle's, so she replied politely, 'Yes, thank you. I slipped and got my foot caught in a puffin hole. Who even knew there were such things?' As soon as she said it she expected some retort about her ignorance, but it didn't happen.

'It's amazing how somewhere in your own country can be more alien than being abroad.'

'Well, quite,' she replied, glancing at Seth for some clue about this new Tashelle.

'Come and sit down, Rich has made some lunch.' Tashelle lead the way to one of the seats.

Henry asked for details of what had happened to her, while everyone listened in. It was only then that Daisy noticed Freja sitting alone next to the trailer, her back to everyone.

'It's good to know you're safe,' Henry said once Daisy had finished her story. 'I was lucky to be near the camp when the fog came down.' He looked around. 'The sky's clearing up pretty well now, but I'm not sure how long it will last.'

'That reminds me. When I was up on How Rise I managed to get a bit of signal and I rang the police in Berwick. They said we're in for some more really bad weather. It's already over Berwick and they can't send anyone to pick us up before it clears.'

Henry nodded. 'I take it you told them about . . . you know.' His head went down.

'I did. They weren't thrilled that we'd removed the evidence from where it was situated, but I did explain we thought it was part of the dig.'

'It is unfortunate,' Henry agreed.

'But I doubt it would yield many clues after all these years.'

Daisy remembered the reason the professor had left the camp earlier. 'Did you find Angus?'

'No, but — ' His eyes narrowed and he cocked his head to one side, as if listening to something.

A moment later they all heard it, the unmistakable rumble of a Jeep, then saw it in the distance as it skirted past Stow Rise. It was soon pulling up the other side of the trailer.

Angus jumped out, in his customary woollen trench coat, and came round to greet them.

'Are you all OK? I'm sorry I haven't been to the trenches the last couple of days. I couldn't get out of bed. Some kind of fever, and I was so tired. I woke up this morning to find the worst of it had gone. I thought I heard someone knocking yesterday, but couldn't do anything about it.'

'I'm sorry to hear that,' Henry said. 'We did call by early yesterday evening.

We were a bit worried when we didn't get an answer.'

None of them had even considered Angus might be unwell. They'd all jumped to conclusions of him either sneaking around or having left for the mainland.

Rich pointed to the Jeep. 'How did you get here in the mist?'

'I know this island like the back of my hand. So, how have you been doing with the trenches?'

Daisy realised this was going to be the horrible moment of revelation.

Henry guided Angus to a chair. 'Take a seat. We have something to tell you.'

'Have you made an important find?' Angus sounded excited, like a child at Christmas.

'We have, in a way, yes.' Henry took the seat next to Angus.

The rest of the team gathered around, even Freja. Daisy took a step back from them, not feeling it was her place to have a part in this, even though she'd discovered the Lady of Sealfarne, as they'd so appropriately named her.

261

Henry coughed and asked, 'Angus, what do you know about what happened to your mother?'

Angus looked confused.

'Only what we discussed in our emails, Professor. She ran away and never came back.' He leant forward, shoulders slumped, like a little boy left at school, waiting for his mummy to turn up long after all the other children had gone home.

Daisy's heart went out to him. It must have been hard for him as a twelve-year-old to be left on this Godforsaken island with a father who, from the descriptions she'd heard, seemed cold. His mother, on the other hand, had sounded sociable and interested in life. Sir James was undoubtedly the one who'd relished living a recluse's life.

'Angus, we found part of a skeleton that we thought, at first, might be Bronze Age. When we found the rest and looked more closely at all of it, we realised it was recent.'

The was a long, painful pause.

Angus slowly rose from his seat, gulping down air as if he were choking.

'What are you saying? That it's my m-mother? H-how could you know?'

He paced rapidly, pulling his hand through his jet hair. Either he genuinely knew nothing about it or he was a good actor.

Henry rubbed his forehead. This must be hard for him too.

'Because, because your mother's rings are on the hand. I remember in particular the uniqueness of the engagement ring, the emeralds and ruby.'

Daisy noticed he didn't mention the bracelet he'd given her being close by. Angus really didn't need to know that.

Angus sat down, doubled over, releasing a strangled moan like a wounded animal.

'How, how could this be?'

Henry shook his head, walking away.

Seth took charge once more.

'Angus, the arm looks like it was broken not long before she — disappeared. Does that ring any bells?'

It looked for a while as if Angus wouldn't reply, then he said in a soft voice, 'She did it falling down one of the cliffs near the castle.' He straightened himself, but still looking at the ground. 'They're quite low there and she landed on the sand. I heard her tell my father she thought she was pushed.'

'It must be catching,' Rich muttered so softly it was unlikely Angus heard him.

'She went to the hospital on the mainland but it was still bandaged when she disappeared. D-do you have any idea how she died?'

Seth nodded. 'We found a wound on the back of her head, as if she'd sustained a blow from something heavy.'

Angus raised his head to observe Seth. 'Do you mean someone hit her with a heavy object?'

'I suppose it's possible she fell and hit her head on a rock. There are plenty around here.'

She was sure Seth didn't believe that, but it might give Angus with a less stark picture for now.

'Oh, no, no . . . ' Angus groaned. 'But if she did fall, how did nobody see her before covering her over with earth? She would have been obvious. No, this was deliberate, I'm sure it was.'

When no one else moved, Tashelle went to him, hunkering down and saying, 'I'm so sorry, Angus. Whatever the whys and wherefores, we're not going to be able to solve any of it at the moment. Daisy's already called the police but they can't get here yet because the weather's pretty bad there and it's heading in this direction. They said hopefully it'll have died down by tomorrow morning and they'll send a team over.'

Angus sniffed and wiped his eyes, then lifted his head. 'I'm sorry. I guess at the back of my mind I always wondered whether my father had something to do with her disappearance. They argued a lot while the archaeologists were here, all those years back, which was unusual. I thought it might stop once they'd all gone, but it didn't. Within four weeks my mother had disappeared.'

'We shouldn't jump to conclusions,' Seth said. 'Would you like something to eat or drink?'

'No, thank you. I'd just like to see her, please.'

'What, the skeleton?' Freja said in horror.

'My mother, all the same.'

The team looked round at each other. Henry was clearly not about to budge. Seth was the first to move. 'Of course. I'll fetch the box. Tashelle, would you help me?'

They brought the two boxes back together to the rock table, placing them carefully down side by side. Seth opened the lid of each, unfolding the fabric lying over the bones.

Angus came forward, halted, took a deep breath then looked into each box in turn. He stood there, looking down a long while before saying, 'Yes, they are my mother's rings.'

'He seems very calm,' Rich whispered to Daisy.

'Probably the shock,' she muttered back.

After a minute Angus turned to them all. 'Thank you for wrapping her up with such care. I dare say the police will want her for some time, but I hope to have her buried on the island, near Eigbech beach, a favourite place of hers.'

'If your father allows you to,' Freja said.

Tashelle glared at her. 'Freja, keep quiet. This is not the time or place.'

'No, it's a good point,' Angus said. 'But I don't think my father would refuse my request. Lady MacKinnon might have something to say, but that's for me to sort out.'

'You don't get on with your step-mother then?' Tashelle asked.

'Let's just say that my mother will always be the only Lady MacKinnon to me. Miss Armstrong, as she was, never liked me much and tries to make my father more indifferent to me than he already is. But enough of that. You must all come to the house tonight. I insist. The weather was horrendous enough last night. You might as well spend your last night on the island in comfort. There are sufficient rooms.'

Seth was about to reply when Henry perked up.

'Thank you, Angus, that's very kind of you. But wouldn't you rather be alone at this time?'

'No, I'd rather have company and something to do to stop me feeling so helpless.'

'In that case, we're happy to accept your offer.'

'I'll give you time to pack and come back at two-thirty, before it starts to get dark. I can take you over in two trips.'

With that he strode back to the Jeep, jumping in and moving off hastily.

'Come along now,' Henry ordered. 'We have an hour and five minutes to pack up. All concentrate on your own belongings first, then we'll take down the tents before packing the rest of it.'

Each of them headed to their tents, except for Daisy who waylaid Seth before he got to his.

'Maybe I'm being paranoid, Seth, but is it really a good idea to stay with Angus? As sorry as I feel for him, it has the air of being herded into one place where we'll be sitting ducks. Tell me I'm just being idiotic . . . please?'

Seth hesitated. 'No, I'm inclined to agree with you, but I'm not sure what else we can do. We're sitting ducks out here, too.'

Henry clapped his hands to get their attention. 'I'll ask you not to mention the mystery incidents to Angus. He has enough to contend with.'

'I agree,' Tashelle said. 'And I can't see he would have any reason to carry them out.'

'Someone did,' Rich muttered.

Daisy let Seth get on, running to her tent to start packing. As odd thoughts began to invade her brain she worked quicker in order to block them out. But one thought wouldn't quite disappear.

Seth was the only one not to be either attacked or suffer because of it . . .

13

Seth and Daisy were part of the second group to be transported from camp to the house. Rich was with them, in the front, discussing the island with Angus. Although he was driving slowly, the rough terrain of slopes and boulders still made the journey uncomfortable. Daisy was sitting in the back with Seth, who was sitting away from her, peering out at the landscape.

He leaned over to whisper, 'I'm sorry about all this. I knew it would be cold and uncomfortable here, and a bit awkward with Tash, but I honestly had no idea it was going to be so dangerous — or that we'd uncover a body.'

'It's hardly your fault. Though I did wonder for a while back there why you'd never been involved in any of the episodes.'

He leaned against the door, his eyes

crinkled with concern. 'You thought it might be me?'

'No, that's not what I meant.' It had flitted across her brain for all of two seconds, but that was all. Trust her to give the wrong impression. 'But it did occur to me that whoever was responsible might want us to *think* it was you. And, if it was one of the group, they may have staged their own attack or broken their own lens ... if it *was* broken.'

'I see. You're right about me not being targeted. That's odd, isn't it?' He turned to look outside. 'We're here. We'll discuss this later.'

He seemed a little put out. Was he brooding on the fact that she'd suspected him? Why couldn't she ever explain anything succinctly?

Angus parked at the front of the castle, next to the trailer transported in the first shift. They each pulled their rucksacks and bags out of the back of the Jeep, then followed Angus to the building.

A shroud of darkness had descended and with it, ominous clouds that made the sky feel low and imprisoning.

'We'll go the back way.'

Angus led the way round the castle and through a gnarled wooden gate into a walled area behind what must once have been a garden.

'My mother used to grow flowers and vegetables here,' Angus said, as if hearing Daisy's thoughts. 'She got wonderful results, given the soil and weather.' It was as if he was speaking about an old lady who'd passed away after a good life.

How old would she have been, Emma MacKinnon? Henry was mid-sixties, so probably about the same. No age at all then . . . even now.

The ancient grey building loomed up in front of them, lights on in every window — in contrast to the last time they visited.

They entered through the kitchen — a neat, clean Victorian-looking room with everything in its place. Copper pots hung from the whitewashed walls above cupboards on one side. On the wall opposite the door was a range. On it, a large pot simmered. In the middle of the room was a table, laid for seven.

Daisy soaked up the warmth of the room. She'd forgotten what it was like not to be always a little chilly. Even with the roaring fires Rich had produced, there had still remained a sense of chill beyond them.

'This way.' Angus headed out of the kitchen.

They entered a large hallway, coming past the side of a wide staircase. The hall consisted of dark wood panels. The dim wall lamps lent an air of mystery to the room.

'You may leave your bags and coats here,' Angus said, pointing to where the others had already abandoned theirs. Ahead were the two tall, solid front doors. They followed Angus diagonally across the hall to another, smaller set of doors. He stood to one side, gesturing them in.

Henry, Tashelle and Freja were already there, relaxing in armchairs in front of the fire.

'Please, sit down. I've prepared a casserole for supper later. There's no cook or any other hired help here over the Christmas holidays, I'm afraid. Now, I'll just go and fetch you some wine. It must have been a harrowing few days for you, out in the cold, discovering ghosts.'

Rich and Seth went directly to the chairs, but Daisy went to look round the room. There was no panelling, as in the hall. Instead the stone walls were bare. The two tall, wide windows had heavy curtains drawn across them.

'The decor is excessively old-fashioned, I know,' Angus said as he removed his coat.

Daisy noticed for the first time that Angus was handsome in a careworn, old-fashioned sort of way. His clothes included a loose shirt and waistcoat, which blended in with the surroundings but were at odds with the laced-up combat boots and jeans.

'I think it's rather charming,' she said. 'Not at all what I expected from the outside, yet at the same time perfectly fitting. It's very . . . tidy.' That was the wrong thing to say, as if she expected it to be chaotic. 'I mean, given the age of it.' No, she was digging herself a bigger hole. 'Sorry, I didn't mean to insult it — or you.'

'Not how I take it at all. I often think it's a shame my father doesn't open up the island and house to tourists. I'm sure its quaintness would prove immensely popular. He once allowed boats to moor on the jetty and observe the varied bird life we have here. But he stopped that after my mother disappeared. No doubt another one of Miss Armstrong's suggestions. Never mind. Please — Daisy, is it?' She nodded. 'Take a seat with the others.'

Daisy went to the fireside, sitting on a wooden chair next to Seth. She smiled at him, but he was looking at the fire.

'I have a rich, red wine I opened

earlier to breathe,' Angus announced. 'I'm sure some of you will appreciate it as much as me.'

He gave out glasses. Nobody declined. It felt slightly bizarre sitting here, in old-fashioned splendour, after what they'd found in Trench 1. It reminded Daisy of something, and when she realised what it was, it unsettled her. It was as if they'd all been dropped into a murder mystery, such as an Agatha Christie.

There you go with that silly imagination of yours. Matt was in her head again. He had no imagination whatsoever.

She held up her glass when Angus got round to her, looking at the ruby liquid and wondering . . . Being daft again. Seth was still distracted as his glass was filled.

When Angus reached Tashelle she smiled coyly. 'Thank you, Angus.' She breathed in the aroma. 'Oh, that bouquet is wonderful. What is it?'

While Angus discussed what he described as a claret she gave him doe eyes, nodding as if she knew exactly what he was talking about. Perhaps she did.

Daisy glanced at Seth who was looking at Henry.

Everyone apart from Freja took a sip. Daisy tasted a drop of the wine. It was fruity and warming, encouraging her to take a proper mouthful. If it was anything dodgy, hopefully it would be a sleeping draught. She could do with a nice snooze, despite it being . . . She looked at the grandfather clock near the door. Five past four, way too early for bedtime.

'That's that bottle done,' said Angus, who had not had any. 'Excuse me while I fetch another.'

As soon as he left the room, Freja said, 'Let's hope this isn't drugged so he can murder us in our beds.'

'Well that's a stupid statement,' Rich snapped. 'If it's drugged we wouldn't even get to bed.'

'You know what I mean. Don't be such a pain.'

'I'm a pain?'

'Do not start this infernal bickering again,' Henry warned. 'We're guests here.'

Freja stood up, walking to a large spider plant near the window. She tipped her wine into the soil and returned to her seat.

'Really, Freja! You're being ridiculous.'

'You won't say that when you're all lying unconscious, or worse, and I've escaped.'

Henry drank his wine down in one go, placing the empty glass on the occasional table nearby. 'There. If there's anything wrong we'll soon know. And that'll be an end to it.'

Outside a clap of thunder ripped through the air. Moments later a torrent of water could be heard hitting stone, glass and rocks.

Freja laughed. 'How poetic.'

Henry sighed. 'And so it begins . . . '

★ ★ ★

Two hours later, they were setting off to the kitchen for dinner, forgoing the dining room which, Angus informed them, would be freezing. Clearly the wine had not been interfered with as Henry, as well as the rest of them, was conscious and well, even if he had become more withdrawn.

As they passed through the hall, Seth drew Daisy back a little, slowing her down until the others had gone ahead. 'Freja . . . ' he started.

'Making rather a point of Angus being guilty of the attacks earlier?' Daisy finished.

'As if trying to deflect suspicion.'

'To be honest, Seth, this whole trip has been full of red herrings. I think we're going to have to play along until either the person who's responsible shows their hand or the police arrive.'

'I suppose you're right. I don't like being helpless. You're not still thinking it could be me?'

She was about to tell him she never really had in the first place when Rich popped his head round the bottom of the stairs. 'Are you two lovebirds coming? It smells good in here.'

They sat together in the kitchen, Daisy at one end of the table, Seth next to her on the long side. Tashelle had placed herself next to Angus, who was at the other end. Everyone seemed hungry enough not to question the lamb casserole they were all tucking into. The odd phrase of appreciation and the occasional request for bread to be passed along the table was the only conversation to break the silence.

The rain was still hammering outside, the thunder interrupting every thirty seconds or so, with the lightning visible through the uncurtained kitchen windows.

'Is this ever going to stop?' Freja whined, dipping a crust into the gravy of the casserole.

'It's got a way to go yet,' Daisy replied, 'if what the police told me over the phone is true. It's not supposed to die out until the early hours.'

'We've seen some storms here,' Angus said, placing his elbows on the table, linking his hands. 'It's as if it's cleansing the land. Tomorrow will be a strange day, the turning over of a new page.'

Tashelle leaned forward, her hand near his arm. Daisy thought for one moment she was going to take hold of it but she didn't. 'I'm sorry it's worked out this way for you. Even after all these years I imagine it's not what you expected.'

'No. The eternal optimist inside me always expected her to turn up again one day, though deep down I feared the worst. In many ways it's a relief. I have some sort of closure. I did wonder if she'd had an affair with someone from the dig and ran away with them. I asked my father once, in my late teens, suspecting he knew but was keeping it a secret. He roared with fury, shouting that he didn't want to talk about it. If she was having an affair, she didn't run away with whoever it was . . . unless his body is here, yet to be discovered.'

'Well Henry,' Freja said. 'Now might

be the time to 'fess up. What do you think?'

Rich nudged her roughly. 'Freja, shut up, eh?'

Angus regarded Henry. 'Do you know anything about this, Professor?'

Henry took a long swig of his wine.

'Angus, your mother didn't have an affair with anyone. She *was* in love with someone, but she chose to stay with James, mostly for your sake. She told me this herself.'

'And who was it?' Angus asked in a way that suggested he'd already guessed.

Henry studied his food.

'I'm sure you've realised it was me, Angus. I've cursed myself every second since we discovered Emma in that trench. I suspected it was her straight away. I couldn't help thinking it was my fault she was there. All those years back, if I hadn't encouraged the friendship and her interest . . . I'm sure your father guessed, and even though Emma chose to stay — '

Angus stood, saying calmly, 'Whatever happened, my mother had a mind of her own. It wouldn't have mattered what you did if she'd set her heart on something. She often did things my father disapproved of — like tending the garden. He said they could afford to hire others to do that. After my mother disappeared, I was sent to boarding school. Miss Armstrong was kept on in the role of housekeeper and ran the place as my father wanted it. But if my father was responsible for my mother's death — and I find it hard to believe he was — I've no doubt it was an accident, done in the heat of the moment.'

Daisy wanted to ask why he wouldn't have just said that at the time. He would have needed to bury the body, and to have done so without Miss Armstrong, or any other hired help, suspecting any-thing.

And what about this small case of belongings that was supposed to have disappeared? It was either premeditated or beautifully organised afterwards. Either way was a crime.

Seth cleared his throat. 'I don't wish

to cause offence, Angus, or any more distress, but I have to ask . . . do you know anything about the assault on the camp, or those on Daisy, Rich, Tashelle and Henry? Could there be someone else lurking about the island?'

'I wasn't attacked, I slipped,' Henry insisted. 'It has nothing to do with Angus, so please, let's leave it. I asked you not to mention it.'

'No, Professor, you mustn't leave it,' Angus said. 'I know nothing about any attacks, but please, do tell me,' he said, sitting again.

Seth quickly explained, with input here and there from some of the others.

When he'd finished, Angus looked puzzled.

'I'm so sorry this happened. I would surely have known if somebody else had landed, with the jetty just outside.'

'But you were ill,' Tashelle pointed out. 'And maybe asleep much of the time?'

Henry stood, his chair scraping across the flagstones. 'All right, all right! I was responsible for the incidents, OK?'

Among wide-eyed glances of indignation, Rich said, 'But why?'

'Because, I suspected straight away that our Lady of Sealfarne was Emma. I didn't like where it was heading, the fuss and media coverage it would cause, the wounds it would open. I wanted to leave Emma in peace. I'm sorry, I only meant to scare you into leaving, not to harm anyone.'

Rich thumped his fist on the table, making his plate jump — along with Daisy next to him.

'I nearly fell down a cliff! And look at my face, all bruised and scratched still.'

'It was only a low cliff,' Henry countered.

Tashelle said, 'Your face? You should see my arms and legs, all scabs where I fell in the gorse.'

'That was unfortunate . . . ' Henry started.

'And my camera lens?' Freja hollered. 'Six hundred pounds that cost me!'

'I really didn't mean — '

'You denied it when Rich asked,' Seth added.

'No, what I said was, do you think I'd do all that merely to take a dig to another university?'

Seth's face was red with fury. 'Twisting your words doesn't make it any less a lie. And you could have hurt Daisy in the — '

'You really are a prize pillock!' Freja interrupted.

Seth scrunched his forehead up. 'And why wet Daisy's tent? That happened before we discovered the remains.'

Tashelle and Freya joined the fray, each voice trying to shout above the other. Daisy couldn't believe the insensitivity of it all, and before her brain had time to veto it, she was shouting above the din, 'Stop it! Everyone, stop it!'

The noise ceased immediately, maybe because they were so surprised it was her shouting. She was surprised, too. She had a moment of self doubt before she ploughed on.

'Do you think this is helping Angus

287

at all? Clearly everyone's upset, but I don't see that shouting over each other is going to sort anything out. At least now we know who's responsible, and we don't need accusations flying yet again.'

Freya pushed her chair back and crossed her arms. 'Much as it pains me to agree with you, you're right. Oh yah, it's all crystal clear. Because why would you want to scare us off, Henry, if you loved Emma? You'd want to find out who did this to her, not leave her in peace, as you put it, her murderer left to roam free. But he has been roaming free . . . hasn't he, Henry?'

Henry placed his head in his hands, rubbing his eyes with his fingertips. 'Why would I do that?'

'Perhaps she'd agreed to leave with you, then at the last minute got cold feet and you got angry.'

'That's enough,' Angus said with quiet authority. 'My mother was still alive after Professor Webb left the island. He can't be responsible. Please, let us finish our meal in peace.'

Freja placed her cutlery in the middle of her plate, despite only having eaten about half her meal. Tashelle regarded her with narrowed eyes from her place opposite. She placed her own cutlery at the sides of her plate before standing and walking around the other side of the table.

Freja ignored her until Tashelle grabbed at something to the side of her — Freja's shoulder bag. Straight away she pulled out a green device that looked like a voice recorder.

'I thought so!' Tashelle growled.

'Give that back!' Freja tried to push her chair back to get out, but her panic hindered her.

'You've been recording us?'

When Freja managed to get up she tried to grab the recorder from Tashelle, who, being six inches taller, held it up too high for her.

'Sit down, Freja,' Seth demanded.

She became still, looking disdainfully at them.

'This trip should have been dynamite

for me — ka-ching! Loads of dosh for a dig full of confrontations, a spectacular find and a body. You lot have ruined it. And yes, I wet Daisy's tent in the hope she'd share with Seth and there'd be a showdown with Tash — but you're losing your edge, Tash.'

She stormed off, leaving the bag and recorder.

'She devises and presents TV shows about archaeology,' Rich explained to Angus. 'Over-dramatised fluff like *History in Your Garden*.'

'Yes, I'm aware of them,' Angus said

'We discovered she was planning one called *When Digs Get Dirty*,' Tashelle added.

Angus tutted. 'I'm sorry to hear that. Tashelle, you did the right thing.'

Tashelle treated him to a beaming smile that at the same time managed to convey sympathy. 'Thank you, Angus. Now, to carry on with your delicious casserole.'

Daisy would have laughed out loud at the obvious play Tashelle was making for Angus, but now was not the time. Out of all the riddles this trip had dug up, one thing was no mystery: Tashelle had some front!

She was about to convey this in an undertone to Seth, especially after their conversation in the hall, but something about the way he was concentrating on the food, head down, ignoring everyone, prevented her.

He was probably regretting bringing her, and wondering how to break it off.

Her plans for her new life seemed pointless now. What a shame when she'd felt so positive about it all. Better to distance herself from Seth before they had to say goodbye. That way it would hurt less.

★ ★ ★

Daisy was having problems dropping off with the rain beating against the windows and the constant lightning. She counted twenty-seven strikes, one after the other. Tashelle, sleeping in the other bed, was gently snoring and oblivious to the noise.

Just her luck to get a twin bedroom with Tashelle, but it could have been worse. Freja was in the single room opposite theirs, next to the bathroom. Angus had the other bedroom on the first floor. The rest of the men were sharing a room on the second floor, next to that belonging to Sir and Lady MacKinnon. It had no beds so they were sleeping on their mats in their sleeping bags. Still, better than being out in this weather.

Daisy drifted in and out of sleep, dreaming about bones and thunder-storms. Matt and Callie featured at some point, though when she woke up she couldn't remember what part they'd played. In another dream, Seth was walking away and she'd felt a profound sense of loss.

The next time she woke, the rain had stopped. She listened for a clap of thunder. Nothing. She sighed with relief. She had no idea of the time and she couldn't be bothered to look. She drifted off to sleep quickly.

When she awoke once more it was still dark. She turned onto her back and stared up into the pitch black. It was then she noticed a new sound. Not wind, not thunder or rain. A boat's motor?

She swivelled round and reached for the bedside table. Finding her phone, she checked the time. Seven fifty-five. Was Angus leaving?

Switching on the torch on her phone, she made her way to the window. Once there she switched off the torch before gently lifting one curtain. Below there was another light, a full-sized torch by the looks of it. The boat sound had ceased. Instead there were voices, though Daisy could tell nothing about them.

She placed the curtain back and switched her phone torch on again to walk back to her bed. There was a sweatshirt she'd left at the end in case she got cold, which she pulled on over her pyjamas. She crept to the door, opening it carefully and not quite closing it behind her.

Tiptoeing past Angus's room, she crept to the top of the stairs and peered through the balustrade, like a child on Christmas Eve. She had a view of the hall but couldn't quite see the front doors as they opened. She turned her torch off just before the hall lights went on.

One male and one female voice became clear. Daisy clung to the balustrade and held her breath. About to get a better look at the new company, she suddenly felt a hand on her arm and heard a hoarse whisper, 'What the hell are you doing?'

14

Daisy jumped, gasping, as she swung around. Behind her was Tashelle, her arms tucked under her armpits over bright pink pyjamas.

Daisy clutched her chest and briefly closed her eyes. 'You scared the life out of me!'

'What are you doing out here, creeping about?'

'Shhh. I heard talking from outside, a man and a woman. It didn't sound like anyone in the group. Come down here — look.'

Tashelle dipped down, peering through the balustrade. 'Oh man, we're in trouble.'

Below, two people were removing water-proofs, and then coats, hanging them up on hooks on the wall. The woman was tall and skinny, with her blonde hair pinned up into a ruffled chignon. The man had abundant grey hair and an ample frame.

'This will be Angus's doing, mark my words,' the woman said. 'Up to some nonsense with his arty friends, no doubt. Look at all this mucky stuff.' She pointed to the waterproofs.

'Let's hope that's all it is, and not some more sinister mischief,' the man replied, his voice deep with a Scottish burr.

They disappeared towards the drawing room.

'Why is Sir James back before schedule?' Tashelle said.

Daisy was concentrating on the hall below and what to do next, so it was a few seconds before she realised Tashelle had started to creep down the stairs. 'What are you doing?' she hissed.

'I'd rather face him head-on than have him trying to murder us in our beds.'

'There won't be any need for that,' came a third voice, as Angus appeared from the gloom, tying up his dressing gown.

Tashelle wrapped her arms around herself, no doubt self-conscious about the pink pyjamas.

'I gather, from what you were saying, that my father has returned. I suggest you fetch the professor and the others, and join us downstairs.'

Daisy nodded, then headed up to the second floor, where she rapped on the men's bedroom door, going in without waiting for a reply.

She clicked the light on. All three men sat up from their sleeping bags, shielding their eyes from the brightness.

'James and Mary MacKinnon have returned. Angus has gone down to face them. He needs some support.'

'Good heavens!' exclaimed Henry, unzipping his sleeping bag revealing purple thermals.

Daisy turned and made her way back downstairs. In her bedroom, she found Tashelle dressed and putting on trainers. When she'd finished she went to the door, but stopped, keeping her eyes averted as Daisy dressed.

'Just to let you know, I only tried to get back with Seth because I was royally ticked off about that berk Anthony dumping me. Imagine, him dumping me! I told him I preferred Seth anyway, just to get back at him, so it seemed smart to try a reconciliation . . . nothing personal. Don't get me wrong, Seth's a great guy, just probably not the best guy for me. Sorry if I came over like a cow.'

'It's OK, I get it,' Daisy said. 'Thanks for explaining.' Not that it mattered now. Seth probably didn't consider himself the best guy for her. She'd blown it with her unintentional accusation. 'Let's go and rescue Angus.'

★ ★ ★

There was already an argument going on when they all reached the drawing room, Sir James and Lady Mary standing with their backs to the fireplace that was filled now only with ash.

Angus said in a raised voice, 'I'm asking you to explain why you would be so bothered about anyone coming here. Even the tour boats aren't allowed to moor up any more. It's not as if the passengers were going beyond the jetty. It can't just be because my mother ran away. What bearing does that have on it?'

Mary took several steps towards Angus. 'Your father does not have to explain his actions to you! Aye, even in your forties you're trouble. We made a snap decision to come home early as we'd had enough of that terrible hotel in Edinburgh, only to find you'd gone behind his back.' She looked to the door. 'Now we're being joined by your so-called friends. Trespassers, the lot of them!'

Her face pinched into a scowl that reminded Daisy of Cinderella's stepmother in a childhood book. It didn't sound as if Angus had told them about the body yet, which was maybe just as well.

Sir James walked past his wife and son to stand in front of the Henry. 'Professor Henry Webb. I should have known. So you thought you'd sneak back here in my absence and carry on with those ridiculous digs. It wasn't enough that you spirited my wife away. Where is she, Henry?'

Henry regarded the rest of his party, maybe wondering how to play this. Seth shook his head very slightly when Henry caught his eye.

'James, I told you then and I'm telling you now, Emma did not run away with me, despite what you think. I haven't seen her in thirty years.'

'Then where did she go? And why come back? To rub my face in it?'

Angus stood between Henry and Seth.

'I invited them, Father. I was interested in the Bronze Age history of this island.'

Mary stamped her booted foot. 'How dare you disobey your father's instructions! You're undisciplined, just like your mother.'

'Mary, please, don't involve her,' James said.

'Why not? She caused nothing but trouble. The professor was taken in by her too. All that sweetness, but she could be a vicious piece of work — and I should know.'

Angus, whose lips had narrowed, clenched his jaw and edged towards her. Before he reached her, his father put out a hand to stop him.

'Don't you talk about my mother like that. You weren't fit to wipe her boots. If there was a vicious piece of work in this house, it wasn't her.'

Mary narrowed her eyes, leaning forward. 'You, in the doorway, what are you up to?'

They all whipped round as one to see Freja stepping carefully in and a little way towards them with her camera, filming. She must have found her camera bag in the men's bedroom.

'What on earth do you think you're doing?'

'Waiting for the confession,' Freja replied.

'Confession to what?' Sir James demanded.

'To the — '

Rich lunged at Freja. 'Give that thing to me!'

Freja was too quick for him, skipping sideways. Daisy saw her chance, sneaking round while Freja was concentrating on Rich. Grabbing her arm in a shoulder lock, Daisy pulled the camera out of her grip. Freja ran after her but was blocked by Seth. Freja put her hands up, as if in surrender, running backwards until she faced Sir James and his wife.

'Get out, all of you!' Mary screamed.

'The confession I'm waiting for is the one from Lady Emma's murderer!' Freja shouted.

'Her what?' yelled Sir James, his face contorted with confusion. 'I don't understand. The police have never contacted me to say her body's been found.'

Mary took hold of his arm.

'They're making it up, trying to scare you.'

'No, no — we're not,' Henry spluttered. 'We found her bones. We thought it was a Bronze Age woman until we came to the hand with the rings. Her engagement ring gave her identity away.

The emeralds and ruby. It was unique. How could you have killed such a beautiful flower?'

Henry was on the verge of tears.

Angus retreated to sit on the seat of the bureau, lowering his head into his hands. James was frozen, with wide eyes and his mouth open.

'Say something,' Henry demanded.

'I — I have no idea what you're talking about. Emma left the island. She even took a case with some belongings, including photos of Angus.'

'How do you know that?'

'I don't believe what you're saying. I demand to see her, to see the ring for myself. And if it's her, how would you know she was murdered?'

'Shall I fetch the boxes?' Tashelle asked.

Henry replied, 'No. Not yet.'

Mary took James's arm, leading him to an armchair. 'Come, sit down. You've had a shock, but it's all stuff and nonsense. Emma ran away, and that's an end to it.'

She looked down her nose at the group, screwing it up as if a smell was offending her.

'Even if there is a body, it could be anybody's. Even the ring proves nothing. Would you really remember it after all this time, Professor Webb? It might be a member of the old archaeology team who got into an argument with another member, and hit their head with the nearest heavy object.'

James nodded. 'Yes, my dear, you could well be right. Don't you think so, Professor Webb?'

'I'd recognise that ring anywhere, because — '

Then something occurred to Daisy.

'Hang on a moment. Nobody mentioned there was a head wound.'

'That's right,' Seth agreed. 'We didn't mention the cause of death.'

'Oh, please, you're trying my patience.' Mary blinked rapidly. 'I just assumed, because it's the most obvious way, of course.'

'What about stabbing or poisoning?'

Daisy suggested. 'Or pushing over a cliff. Drowning? No, it's not obvious at all.'

Angus lifted his head and glared at his stepmother. Slowly he stood, his mouth opened to speak, but whatever he was going to say, James beat him to it.

'Mary, did you kill Emma?'

She slowly backed away. 'Of course not.' She released a small laugh that mocked the idea. 'But I wouldn't blame anyone for doing so. She thought far too much of herself.'

Sir James stood. 'It was you who told me the case and items were missing, that she'd run off with Henry. But that's a lie, isn't it?'

'What else was I to do?' she gasped. 'I knew Emma was in love with Henry. I was banking on her running away. But she chose not to, because of Angus.' She spat out her former pupil's name. 'She was going to sack me, told me I inter-fered too much in Angus's upbringing and the running of the home.' She seemed to be talking to herself now, not anyone in the room. 'You were going to make a new start, she said — away from this lovely island. I couldn't have that now, could I?'

The clock chimed once. Daisy glanced over to it. Half past eight. In the brief diversion the clock brought, Mary ran from the room, reaching the door before anyone could grab hold of her.

Daisy emerged into the hall in time to see her turn both handles of the front door. She was about to bolt out when she was faced with a wall of four people.

The police had arrived.

Mary shouted, 'Thank goodness you're here! These people found the body of my husband's late wife, and I think my husband murdered her!'

Daisy came forward, clutching Freja's camera.

'Nice try, but I didn't turn the camera off. It was still running and caught your confession.'

'Nice one, Daisy!' Tashelle said, high-fiving her. 'And nice one, realising no one had mentioned the head wound. Didn't even occur to me.'

'Great work, Daisy,' Seth said, not moving towards her. 'It's sad it happened, but at least we have the answer to both mysteries, and Angus and his father will get proper closure. Go to him, Tashelle. I think he'd appreciate your support.'

She left without waiting for Seth's reply.

When everyone else had left the hall, Seth explained quietly to Daisy, 'When you all went to bed last night, Angus was asking about Tashelle, whether she was in a relationship, what she did . . . '

'Wow! Be sure to keep me up to date on that situation — ' She gasped. No, that statement assumed too much, and she was sure it wasn't on offer. 'You know . . . through Callie and Dave,' she added. That was better. No expectations.

'Though Callie and Dave . . . Yeah, OK.'

He walked away towards the drawing room.

So that was that. She'd been right. If he'd been interested in taking the relationship any further, that was his opportunity to say something. So it was back to London and the biology degree, and boredom.

15

Seth and Daisy stood at the back of the boat, watching as Sealfarne Island slowly became smaller. The sun was shining on it now and birds keened overhead.

'Wonder if we'll ever go back there?' Seth called above the engine noise, realising immediately that although there was an outside chance he'd go back, Daisy was highly unlikely to. He'd completely blown it with her, bringing her here to danger. If he'd had any doubts before, her announcement that he could let her know about Tash and Angus through Callie and Dave confirmed it.

'Who knows? Sir James might be grateful to the archaeology team for uncovering the mystery. Or he might just want to forget the whole incident.'

'You couldn't blame him.'

Seth wondered if this was Daisy's wish too, to forget this whole incident.

'You're going to your parents' for New Year?'

'Yes.' Daisy sighed. 'That world seems so far away at the moment.'

She clearly regretted that state of affairs.

'Soon it'll seem normal, and this will feel like a million miles away. Still, you got a taste of what it's like to be an archaeologist,' Seth said. No, that won't help. 'That is, finding the artefacts and trying to puzzle things out, not the other bit. Though that'll be something to tell your grandchildren, I suppose.'

Sometime in the future when she'd have forgotten him completely . . .

Sadness filled his chest and he felt he could hardly breathe. Seeing her off on the train from Alnwick was was going to be one of the hardest things he'd ever done.

Daisy leaned her arm on the washboard.

'I imagine it's quite exciting, all the same.'

'I don't suppose your biology degree will ever be quite this eventful.' He laughed, though he didn't feel like it.

'You're not wrong there. That's why I was wondering . . . ' She paused. 'This is going to sound really daft.'

He felt his pulse quicken. What was coming? He didn't want to raise his own hopes. 'Go on.'

What she said next came out all in a rush.

'I was thinking of swapping degrees, you see, to do archaeology. To give up the biology, and start again in September. If I'm not too late to apply, that is . . . to your university.'

Of all the things Seth was expecting to hear, it wasn't that! The surprise must have shown more than he'd intended.

'Oh, I knew I was being ridiculous,' she said, disappointment showing in her furrowed brow and downturned mouth.

'No, not at all,' he said quickly, before she changed her mind. 'I'm just taken aback . . . and rather thrilled, actually. Wow — go for it!'

She regarded him, nibbling at her

bottom lip for a moment. 'Are you sure? You're not just saying that so you don't upset me?'

'Not at all. To be honest, I thought you'd gone off archaeology — and me . . .'

'Oh gosh, no!'

She threw her arms around his neck and kissed him enthusiastically.

'I thought for a moment you'd hate the idea.'

'Quite the opposite. I was worried about how and when I'd see you again. This is the best news I've had all year!' He smiled and she did too, a wide, beautiful smile that lit up her face. He couldn't resist kissing her again.

'Oh, get a room,' Tashelle grumbled, as she came out of the cabin.

Daisy pulled a face. 'What do you think she'll make of me rocking up at your uni?'

'I think she'll have her own preoccupations.' Seth couldn't see how it would work out for Tashelle and Angus, but he hoped it would. 'She won't be on your case any longer, anyway.'

'You can be on my case as much as you like.'

Seth took hold of her hand and they watched Sealfarne Island disappear into the distance.

16

Daisy sat at the kitchen table pondering what to write on the label of the Christmas present. Her mum was busy preparing something for supper, singing along to the radio. Daisy realised her mum was now singing *Last Christmas*.

What was she doing last Christmas? As if she could ever forget the dig at Sealfarne Island. So much had happened this year, so much had changed.

She thought about Mary MacKinnon, and the trial they'd been on standby to give evidence at. They hadn't had to in the end because she'd pleaded guilty and was now in prison.

The group at the dig, including her, had discussed bringing charges against Henry for assault, but in the end decided there was little point. He'd retired and his place as head of department went to one of the older professors.

'Are you going to write that label or just look at it?' her mum asked.

'What shall I put?' She thought for a second before writing *To Seth, A Very Happy Christmas — a bit different to Last Christmas!* She added it to the pile nearby. It included presents for Callie, Dave, Bea and Toby, who were popping down on Boxing Day.

The door from the hall opened and Seth crept in. 'Sorry, that was Rich. Said he got confirmation of his promotion to senior lecturer.'

Daisy clapped her hands. 'That's great!'

'Quick coffee before we head off to Christingle, Seth?' Daisy's mum smiled broadly. She'd really taken a shine to Seth, as had her dad. Neither had been that bothered about Matt.

'Yes please, Mrs Morgan.'

'Kate, please. Goodness, this is going to be a very different Christmas for you both to last year.'

Daisy laughed, since that was what she'd just been thinking. Maybe the song had made her mum think of it too.

'So what's the latest on Sealfarne and Angus? His father left to live on the mainland, you said?'

Seth nodded. 'That's right. Sir James said he didn't want to live with the memories. Angus, on the other hand, wants to make something positive out of it, and allowed the boat trips back last summer. He's in the process of turning the castle into a guesthouse.'

'And he's allowed the archaeology team back,' Daisy added, 'which Tashelle is heading up. That's handy for her, given she and Angus's relationship seems to be going quite strong.'

Kate looked concerned. 'Getting on all right with her now, are you?'

'I am. It's weird having her as a lecturer — and Seth and Rich, but she seems to have me marked out as a star student, which is a bit embarrassing.'

Daisy raised her eyes and tutted, but really she was pleased at how it had all turned out.

'You *are* a star student.' Seth put his arm round her.

'Why, thank you!'

Kate made the coffee and brought it to the table, sitting to join the other two.

'I noticed there's an episode of that *History in Your Garden* on the TV today.'

'Must be an old one,' Daisy said. 'Freja was sacked by the TV company.'

'What happened to her?'

'Back to lecturing, but this time a uni in Dorset. I think Henry might even have written her a reference,' Daisy said.

'Yes, he did,' Seth confirmed. 'I'm not sure I would have after all those stunts, but I guess after us not bringing any charges against him, he wanted to give her a second chance too.'

'So remind me Seth, where are your parents this Christmas?' Kate asked.

'Mexico. But of course they're coming back for New Year, which they haven't done for four years, and my sister and her family are coming over too. It'll be nice for Daisy to meet them.'

'And scary!' said Daisy.

Kate looked at her watch. 'We'd better get our coats on. Dad and Hannah said they'd meet us at the church.'

They all rose and went to the hall. Daisy opened the front door to look out.

'Oh, wow, it's snowing quite heavily now.'

Seth wrapped a scarf round his neck. 'At least we didn't have to cope with that last year.'

'No, because cold, rain, fog and a couple of mega thunderstorms weren't enough,' Daisy joked as she did up her coat.

'Point taken.'

The three of them stepped out and trudged to the gate. Seth opened it, letting them out first.

On the other side of the road, a couple passed, arm in arm. The man turned round and waved.

It was Matt. Daisy waved back.

'He didn't hang around, considering he asked you to marry him only a year ago,' said Kate.

'I'm glad he's found someone else. They're getting married in the spring.'

Seth caught them up. 'Was that Matt?'

'It certainly was.'

'Any regrets at turning him down last year?' He raised his eyebrows.

Daisy laughed. 'You know the answer to that by now,' she said firmly.

Seth smiled, linking his arm through Daisy's as the snow settled all around them.

We do hope that you have enjoyed reading this large print book.

Did you know that all of our titles are available for purchase?

We publish a wide range of high quality large print books including:
Romances, Mysteries, Classics
General Fiction
Non Fiction and Westerns

Special interest titles available in large print are:
The Little Oxford Dictionary
Music Book, Song Book
Hymn Book, Service Book

Also available from us courtesy of Oxford University Press:
Young Readers' Dictionary
(large print edition)
Young Readers' Thesaurus
(large print edition)

For further information or a free brochure, please contact us at:
Ulverscroft Large Print Books Ltd.,
The Green, Bradgate Road, Anstey,
Leicester, LE7 7FU, England.
Tel: (00 44) **0116 236 4325**
Fax: (00 44) **0116 234 0205**

Other titles in the
Linford Romance Library:

HEARTS AND FLOWERS

Vivien Hampshire

Though her former partner is completely uninterested in his unborn child, heavily pregnant Jess can't wait to meet her new baby. However, she hadn't planned on going into early labour at the local garden centre! After baby Poppy arrives, the manager Ed visits the pair in hospital, and they strike up a friendship. Ed finds himself falling for Jess — but can't quite bring himself to tell her. Will the seeds of their chance encounter eventually blossom into love between them?

WHAT THE HEART WANTS

Suzanne Ross Jones

Alistair is looking for a very particular kind of wife: a country girl who would be happy to settle down to life on his farm in the small town of Shonasbrae. Bonnie, fresh from the city to open her first of many beauty salons, isn't looking for a husband and she certainly isn't accustomed to country life. With such conflicting goals, Alistair and Bonnie couldn't be less compatible. But romance doesn't always make sense, and incompatible as the two are, they don't seem to be able to stay apart . . .